AUG 2 5 2022

D1042254

NEW TO LIBERTY

a novel

DEMISTY D. BELLINGER

The Unnamed Press
Los Angeles, CA

To my husband and best friend Neal,
who helped make this possible.

TABLE OF CONTENTS

NEW TO LIBERTY

PART 1
1966

I woke up with nothing ahead of me but road, nothing to the right of me but a dusty grain-filled field, and nothing to the left of me but more field and the profile of Ezekiel, his high forehead gleaming blue from the tint at the top of the windshield. I closed my eyes again so he wouldn't notice that I was awake yet. Carefully, I lifted one of my thighs slowly and just a little, but it stuck quick to the leather seat of his brand-new Sixty Special sedan. The tight Levi's cutoff jean shorts squeezed my pelvic bone, and beads of sweat dotted my belly along the waistband, which collected in a small pool in my belly button. I must have made a noise trying to reposition my thigh, because Ezzy said aloud, "Welcome to Seward County."

"Seward County, Kansas?" I asked. I opened my eyes wider. The sun beamed through the windshield, shading right into my eyes. I squinted and reached for my sunglasses on top of the dash. "Where you grew up?"

"E-yup."

I put the sunglasses on and squinted against the glare. The fields and the long stretch of road were now amber tinted. It was hot enough for the heat devils to play on the paved surface. Tall grasses swayed outside like California palm trees. Every so often, cows or sheep stood stupidly in fields and looked at Ezzy's car speeding by as if it were an oddity. Dilapidated houses and farm buildings were bleached bone gray, and what little paint remained on these structures peeled like birch bark. "Feels like home at all?" I asked.

"About as hot."

"And the air conditioner's on. Shit."

"Don't talk like that. Unbecoming of a lady."

"Shit," I repeated. "No wonder you don't talk much. It's nothing to talk about here but corn or the weather, and the weather is just plain hot."

"That's wheat."

"Corn. Wheat. They both make bread. Where are we going in all this?"

"A little farther west, then we'll find the road the homestead's on."

"You think she'll have air?"

"I know she won't."

"Of course she won't. Shit."

"Don't cuss, Sissily. It is unbecoming."

"It's unbecoming to be in this heat." I picked up my magazine and fanned myself. Because he was older than me, Ezzy thought he could tell me what to do. He didn't want to fly because he wanted me to see America. He wanted to teach me something on this trip, which is another hazard of being with an older man. They can't get it out of their heads that they are responsible for you. I think it was a little of that sense of responsibility, a little of my wanting to get away from a home that I thought I knew, and a little of the money thing. Ezzy was rich. He had money to get a new Cadillac car whenever he wanted to. My family had a little money, but nothing like Ezzy's. The Cadillac we traveled in still smelled like leather just tanned. And that whole trip, I could not eat in the car lest one french fry fall on his precious seats.

"You have something decent to change into before we get there?" he asked. He looked at me quickly as he drove, assessing my clothes.

"I think I do look pretty decent."

"Be serious for a minute, will you?"

"I have a dress." I shifted in my seat and looked straight ahead. Nothing. I pulled down the visor and looked into the mirror. A pimple was forming itself under my left nostril. There were whiteheads on my nose. On my chin, against the left side, was a huge zit. But I had big gray eyes with dark lashes. I had olive skin that easily bronzed in the sunlight. And I had a body that convinced men to leave their wives, which is what Ezzy did.

"Covers much?" he asked.

"Enough," I said. I sighed. "It's so hot." I closed the mirror and sat back in my seat. The leather felt moist against my bare back. Or maybe my back was moist.

"Don't keep repeating it," Ezzy said.

"Why can't we open a Pepsi, huh? I'm dying, Ezzy, baby, it's just too much."

"Just a couple miles more."

"But, Ezzy! Where am I going to change my dress?"

He looked at me again. He looked like a shark and not just the figurative business shark. His forehead was high and jutted out noticeably. His eyes were wide and set wide apart. Icy looking. His nose was somewhat broad but more pointy than wide. His blond hair was lightly pomaded, brushed back. And his mouth seemed full of teeth. He confided to me that he had them all capped.

"Let's get you changed now." He pulled hard to the right and slowed the car on the shoulder. "Know directly where that dress is?"

"Yes, sir."

"Don't call me that. It makes me feel old." Ezzy brought the car to a stop and cut the engine. He reached down beneath the dash and popped the trunk of the car.

I got out of the Brougham Special, the door beeping at me when it opened. I slammed the door as best I could against the hill and the wind. Ezzy was out soon after me.

"Watch the door," he said. "It closes as easy as a baby sleeps. No need for slamming it."

I rolled my eyes and made my way to the trunk. My valise was on top, distinctive in its pinkness. I pulled it to the edge and opened it. I had a gingham dress. It was cool and country looking, something I thought Ezzy's mother would like. I laid it out in the trunk as if I were laying it out on a bed. I peeled off my cutoff shorts. Then Ezzy was behind me, kissing my neck. He ran his hands up and down my belly and hips. I could feel him getting hard.

"We'll never get there if you keep that up," I said.

"Hard not to keep it up around you. Want to christen the back seats?"

When we finished, I wiped the best I could with filler station paper napkins. Then, still in my underwear (I forgot to bring a bra since the only other thing I packed were halter tops), I climbed out of the back seat and made my way to the trunk. Right when I cleared the rear of the car and was facing the trunk, an old work truck with INTERNATIONAL writ big across the grille made its way by. I got goose bumps.

"Shit," Ezzy said. "Mama may have seen us before we her. It was going pretty fast, though, wouldn't you say?"

He was leaving the back seat himself, zipping up his jeans as he walked toward me. From his oxford shirt, which he carried in the hook of his arm, he dug out a cigarette.

"No. I'm sure she saw the bumps around my nipples."

"Shut up, you." He lit the cigarette and looked toward where the truck went. "Could have been worse. Could have been the tractor."

I pulled the dress over my head and straightened it out around me. "Nothing she hasn't seen before."

"You know that don't matter. Seen my undershirt?"

I looked up and saw his A-shirt resting between the rear passenger's seat's headrest and window. I pointed it out. Ezzy worked his way around to the back seat again. He grabbed the shirt and put it on. Next, he put on his holster, which he called "city-slicker lopsided" since it was made for just one gun, then his oxford shirt.

"You look like a real cowboy, you know? Those tight jeans and the pointy-toe boots? Really does it for you."

"And you in that dress, a real cowgirl. Let's go, Sissily."

"Can I drive?"

He laughed. "No! Of course not."

I must have given him a look, because he said, "Do you even have a license to drive?" I shrugged. "Come on, Sissily, I would never let anyone drive my Caddy. Now let's go."

We made our way back into the car. I thought it'd smell like us, but the overwhelming smell of new-car leather overtook all intruding odors. "I don't understand why we are going here again. It's kind of out of the way and there's nothing to see."

"Nothing? Don't you want to see where I come from?" Ezzy said. He was adjusting his seat. He was rechecking his mirrors.

"Why do we have to do this now?"

Ezzy sighed. "Look, I ain't seen my mama in years, okay? Not since I graduated from college."

"That long?"

"Yeah, I got a job out east and never could see my way back. I'd write or call, but I always flew, so I never stopped to see her. Never made a special trip. Maybe that's why she didn't want me to go to school in the first place; she knew that I wouldn't come back."

I looked at Ezzy head-on and he looked weary, worried by my questions. I should have stopped asking him things about himself, but I wanted to know more. "What's she like?" I asked. "How old is she?"

"What difference does it make?"

"Because I want to know how old you are. I could guess if I knew hers."

"Again, it doesn't make a difference."

"So your mother's a farmer?"

"Rancher. They started off farming. Hell, everyone started off farming."

"What's the difference between ranching and farming?" I asked.

Ezzy laughed at me.

"It's so hot!" I lunged for the air conditioner dials to turn the fan on higher, but Ezzy was quicker. He laughed again and blocked my hand from his instrument panel.

"Not a chance," he said.

"It's not like summer in New York. Jesus Christ, it's not even like Memphis! There are no trees anywhere. We'll bake before we get there." I looked out the window at more fields. Even the grasses looked gray.

"But we're there now." Ezzy turned left onto a road that immediately went from pavement to gravel to dirt. Regardless of the promised smooth ride of a Caddy, we bounced in our seats over the rough road. I swallowed air. I felt afraid but didn't know why. We continued up that road for about a good mile. To the left and right of us, the whole way, wheat. I could smell it through the vents of the car. I could smell diesel exhaust, too, from the tractors and other farm vehicles in the area. And I could smell manure. I started getting the feeling that I was much too young for what was about to take place, this reunion between Ezzy and his mother. I don't know what made me feel that way. The only thing I could think of was the haze in the air hanging heavily in the dwindling late-afternoon sunlight. Undoubtedly, the haze came from the wheat and dust from the road. I told myself that.

I was looking straight ahead of me, wanting to see Ezzy's homestead before it me, when I saw three rabbits running alongside the road. "Look," I said, "bunnies!"

Ezzy sucked his teeth. I looked over at him and couldn't tell if he saw the rabbits or not. He confused me, with his New Yorker exterior and cowboy insides. But, of course, that is what made him attractive. His mysterious nature is partly why I left Tennessee and the precarious life I had there to join him in New York, then agreed to take a road trip with him to California. I stared at him, wondering about his thoughts of home, watching the bones and muscles of his jaw clench and unclench.

Then a grayness came into sight just outside his window. A brittle barn, clapboard sided and leaning left-ward, sat in the beaming sun amid what I took to be wild wheat. Next to the barn was an unused silo shooting from the weeds and leaning slightly toward the barn. Not far from it, four cars from when Ford was still alive rusted in the dirt. Last was the house, a large stucco-sided A-frame with extension after extension and sagging roofs. There were too few windows for so much wall. Fiberglass insulation peeked through the cracked stucco. Decades upon decades of the same color of paint covered the sidings, matching the same lovely shade of drab as the barn and silo. But most disturbing was the large person standing in front of the house.

If I didn't know better, and if not for her sizable chest, I would have guessed Ezzy's mother to be a man. But I'd seen a picture of her, though taken in younger years. I'd heard about her. Now she stood outside of her house, in front of the porch, looking as gray as the buildings that surrounded her. But she was much sturdier.

Ezzy slowed considerably and swung the car around. He let it coast to a spot near the house. He cut the engine and sat there for a minute, not looking at me, his childhood home, or his mother. He didn't seem to be looking at anything. "I really want a cigarette," he said. His voice was flat as well water.

"Well, why don't you have one?" I asked. Ezzy turned to me, and I refrained from asking any other questions. He stared at me for a short while, then looked over my shoulder at his ranch, at his mother.

"Wait there. I'll come around and open the door for you." He spoke slowly as if he were giving instructions to someone who would have a hard time understanding him. This worried me more. I nodded to let him know that I got it. He got out of the car and walked the long way around to the passenger-side door.

I noticed I was sweating even more. It dripped from my forehead, down my face, onto my lap. I quickly looked in the mirror affixed to the visor. Beads of sweat dotted my forehead, nose, and upper lip. I didn't want to do this. I was nineteen years old and should have been anywhere else. I should have been, I thought, at least back in Memphis, on someone's veranda, sipping something sweet and cold. Or maybe at someone's pool with my toes dipping in the water. If I was to be meeting anyone's mother, it should have been of a friend, or of a much younger woman who shared an apartment with her husband in Manhattan and summered on the Cape in Massachusetts or in Rhode Island. I shouldn't be in Seward County, Kansas. I wasn't even sure where that was. And Kansas was as storybook dreary as it was in *The Wizard of Oz*.

Ezzy opened my door. "No cussing, remember. And please, mind your manners."

I took out a tissue from the glove box and blotted my face. I turned to Ezzy and gave him my sweetest smile. "I'll put on my best performance."

He smiled back. It came quick but moved slow. His face opened up, and the lines that enhanced his cheeks around the dimples made him look beautiful. I forgot all my complaints and got out of the car.

Mrs. Svoboda stayed put in front of her home. We had to walk to her from the car to meet her. The first thing I noticed about her physically, when we got right next to her, was how tall she was. She was right at Ezzy's height, and he stood over a foot taller than me. She didn't say hello first, or shake my hand, or anything. Instead, she hugged Ezzy as if it were her duty. She didn't smile. I couldn't tell if she was happy to see him or me.

"This isn't Becky," she said, still not saying hello.

"No, Ma, this here is Sissily. I told you about her a few times in the letters I sent."

"Couldn't be much older than Becky," Mrs. Svoboda said.

Ezzy cleared his throat. I stood there, feeling cool under Mrs. Svoboda's gaze and trying hard not to turn on my heel and tell Ezzy that I'd wait in the car.

"She's too dark to be Becky."

I don't know if I reacted, but I grew hot at her remark. I wanted to look at Ezzy to see what he thought. I opened my mouth, but Mrs. Svoboda kept speaking.

"Did you bring any bags," she asked, "or is what you wearing all you got?"

"We have bags," Ezzy said. He took a step toward the car but stopped when his mother spoke again:

"Because it seems I seen that girl there changing on the side of the road," she said.

Ezzy stood still, one foot in the air, ready to take another step. "I wanted her to appear decent for you, Mama."

"Suppose you wanted the same for yourself, too, because I think I saw you changing out there, Ezekiel."

"Suppose I did. I had on a T-shirt while I was driving. Hot, you know."

"Ain't that big ole car got air? That girl couldn't be a year older than—"

"That's it, Mama, that's enough." Ezzy continued walking toward the car.

Mrs. Svoboda asked, "Don't she know about Becky?" to her son, then she turned to me. "You know about Ezekiel's oldest daughter? You know he got a daughter your age?"

"Yes," I said. My voice embarrassed me. It was quiet— soft, which it wasn't usually—and scratchy. And did I call her "ma'am"? "Missus"? "Miss"? Did I dare call her by her first name or "Mama"? "I have met Becky." I cleared my throat, but I knew it would do no good. My mouth felt dry, and Mrs. Svoboda's stare encouraged phlegm to form.

"You went to school with her?" she asked.

"No," I said. "Ma'am," I added, just in case. "Ezzy introduced us."

"Ezzy."

"Yes, ma'am."

"Buzi's son wasn't Ezzy. Ezekiel is my son's name, just as Buzi's son was Ezekiel in the Bible. You read it much?"

"Yes, ma'am."

"Well then, you're a contradiction. If you read the Bible, you'd know enough to not go around breaking up homes. Whoring on the side of the road with my son. My only surviving son."

I looked down at my toes. I listened to her accuse me of all kinds of sins until Ezzy slammed the Brougham's trunk hard. I knew him before he bought that car, and he didn't even slam the ashtray shut, let alone a door or a trunk. This act of aggression I took as sympathy. I considered it heroic.

"That marriage," Ezzy said loudly and tiredly, "was over well before Sissily came along. I thank you, Mama, not to harass the girl."

Mrs. Svoboda shook her head slightly, sucked her teeth loudly in a tsk, and asked, "Do you want dinner?"

Politely, I said yes. "I am starving."

"You don't know what starving is," Mrs. Svoboda said.

I opened my mouth to say something in response, but closed it quickly when I could think of nothing. I tried to look to Ezzy, but he was not in my field of vision. Yet, I didn't want to look away or, worse, look down in defeat. I felt I had lost some kind of round with this woman, and I wanted to stand my ground. I chose to smile at her. "Of course, ma'am," I said quietly.

DEMISTY D. BELLINGER

Ezzy cleared his throat. I looked to see that he was right behind us, looking impatient. "Should we go inside? Get out of the heat?"

Mrs. Svoboda, all battle ready, turned like a soldier. Ezzy came closer to me and nudged me softly on the shoulder, and I obediently followed his mother. He brought up the rear.

The porch was splintered and its stairs creaked as we climbed them. I could hear what I assumed to be chickens clucking, but couldn't see birds of any kind when I looked around. I could also hear the tall grasses rustling in the heavy prairie winds. And I marveled to myself at how that wind brought no respite from the heat, just more hot air blowing around.

Inside, an old red hound dog lay in the corner. When he heard us come inside, he jumped up as much as his body would allow him to, and he walked in step with his mistress. He had this constant whine wheezing out of his nose that whistled in harmony with the blowing wind outside. Eventually, Mrs. Svoboda kicked the dog in his side and ordered him away. She didn't seem to have a name for him.

Everything about the Svoboda house was in ill re-pair. The screen door deterred no insect from flying or crawling inside. The kitchen, the first room we entered, had floorboards that were cracked, warped, and dull. Some parts of it still had some varnish from a vain past, which caused uneven shininess. The walls all over the house were caked thick with touch-up after touch-up of eggshell white. And the newest piece of furniture was probably from the 1930s. Still, Mrs. Svoboda kept it clean. Everything was in its place, the floors were swept, the curtains and furniture dusted. She had a table set nicely for four in her dining room with colorful glass dishes, the kind everyone's mother and grandmothers won at county fairs or got with stamps during the Great Depression.

"You want to see your room now, miss? You will be sharing a bed with me."

My stomach lurched a little. I couldn't imagine that. My answer must have been delayed, because we had stopped walking through the rooms. Mrs. Svoboda and Ezzy were looking at me, waiting for me to say something. In the silence, I could hear Mrs. Svoboda's breathing, heavy and raspy. It was a desperate breath. "What?" I said.

"Do you want to drop that bag of yours off in my bedroom? Where you'll be sleeping?"

"Yes. Please."

Mrs. Svoboda sighed, and her rough breathing filled the air around us. She shifted her weight and turned away from me, continued through the house. I followed her, but Ezzy dropped off from the procession and went into another room.

Her bedroom was small but empty. She had only a bed, a chest of drawers, and a bedside table with a medical ventilator on it. The bed was full-sized with a modest four-poster maple bedframe. There was an old summer quilt on the bed, too. "Set your bag anywhere, miss."

"Sure," I said. "Please call me Sissily."

I walked to the side of the bed that did not have the table beside it and quietly set my bag on the floor. "Ezzy— I mean Ezekiel—didn't stop for food for over four hours."

"I forgot. You said you were starving, right?"

I smiled. She was being sarcastic in a slightly congenial way. Nice.

23

"Well, we'll be eating directly. I can see why my son wants you—chasing his dying youth. But why do you want to be with an old man like him?"

I had prepared for that question. "He is a very interesting person," I began, "and very intelligent. And we both love to travel."

"Oh, don't give me that. It's his money, isn't it?" But she had pronounced "isn't it" as *i-in-it*. "You're what they call a gold digger, right?"

I answered slowly. "No, ma'am. My family has its own money."

"Why are you so dark? Italian? Or is it something else?"

I shrugged. When I blinked my eyes, I saw my mother and father, pleading with me to stay, trying to get me to understand how I came to be, all without telling me much.

Mrs. Svoboda looked closer at me, moving in until she was but an inch away. She studied my face. "Indian? Negro in you?"

I had nothing to tell her. She wouldn't stop staring. "My family's been in America long enough. Maybe there's some Indian."

"This world, I tell you. Is it the sex? That why you and my boy are together?"

"You said that you had food ready?"

She acquiesced. "That I do. I hope you like country cooking. You ain't from New York. Your accent is somewhere else."

"I'm from Tennessee originally."

"Originally. You seem like you've been around. Well, get ready for supper."

I followed her back into the dining room, where Ezzy sat at the table. The hound was in a corner, whining in his sleep. Ezzy looked tired and scared. I could see different lines drawn through his cheeks, lines I hadn't noticed before. He looked really old there, but at his youngest, of course, because he was in his mother's house, which made him appear small and powerless. He had to follow her rules, which included not smoking or sharing a bed with me. With a woman like Mrs. Svoboda as a mother, Ezzy had no choice but to grow into the strong, quiet type—her presence commanded silence.

I slid in across from Ezzy after she told me to have a seat. Mrs. Svoboda left us alone for a while as she went to get the food from the kitchen. "I don't think I wanted to go home before now," I said.

"What? You want to go home?"

"No. No, I don't think so."

"It's just one night, Sissily."

"I said that I didn't think so."

"Well, good, because I ain't driving you back. Of course. And I ain't sending you back." He rubbed his temples with the thumb and forefinger of one hand. I crossed one leg over one knee. Then I switched it around. When Mrs. Svoboda came in with the food, I uncrossed them entirely and slid my knees under the table. Sat up straight.

The meal was as follows: Steel flatware audibly scraped the Depression glass plates. Mrs. Svoboda breathed thickly through her emphysema. Ezzy released a barrage of hesitant sighs as he tried not to speak, tried to speak. The dog's whining ruled over the far left corner of the dining room, and through the windows, the wailing of the wind across the plains whispered in. The dust long settled from thirty years ago came in from the outdoors, stirred over our silence. I fancied I heard it scraping against the old maple floors. It could sand the floors smooth. And from me was probably no sound at all. I tried to breathe so quietly that both Mrs. Svoboda and Ezzy would forget that I was there. I ate with a tentative fork, scraping the tines over the peaks the food formed. I placed the fork on the middle of my tongue to avoid tapping my teeth. It worked. No one looked at me.

The food was almost indescribable. I couldn't tell what it was that I ate. It was something more midwestern than I'd ever had. It involved corn, meat, and something green that seemed added on for show, for my benefit. I think the meat was beef. The food was seasoned only just so, just enough. To drink, we had a tall jar of iced water and a Depression glassful of sweet tea.

Overnight was too long for me to keep silent. It was too tense for me to not talk, so I thought I should bring up something innocuous enough that would not raise any more grief about Ezzy's ex-wife and his kids. I couldn't think of anything to talk about. Nothing eventful happened on our trip that I'd want to share with Mrs. Svoboda, but then I remembered the rabbits we saw not far from the Svoboda homestead. "Ezekiel and I saw some rabbits not too far from here," I said.

Ezzy cleared his throat loudly.

"Probably was jackrabbits," Mrs. Svoboda said.

"Beg your pardon?" I asked. I thought she meant something else, some legendary and mythical creature, like a jackalope. I was hoping that she did say something like that, like she was trying to get one over on a city girl, and then it would prove she was normal.

"A jackrabbit," she repeated.

Ezzy cleared his throat again.

"Excuse me," Mrs. Svoboda said. She stood and left the room. Then I felt horrible. I looked to Ezzy for some sort of clue for what I had done by mentioning rabbits, but he was looking down at his green plate, shoveling midwestern goulash down his throat. I reached one of my legs over to him, touching his foot with my toe. He didn't look up. In the next room, his mother opened drawers and closed them. I could hear her shuffling through papers and other things. I imagined her looking for a rabbit-shooting gun, taking that old hound next to her and going to find those three poor bunnies. Of course, a gun wouldn't fit in the drawers. Maybe she was just looking for the bullets.

Mrs. Svoboda had stopped looking. She slammed a drawer triumphantly. She returned with some pictures, black and white and stiff like ancient photographs from the turn of the century. She handed me one. Someone had written on the back the date: *January of 1934*. The picture was gruesome: men young and old, as well as some young boys, dotted the photo near rows and rows of dead rabbits. The pictured rabbits were shades of gray and lighter gray mottled with splotches of charcoal. *That's blood*, I thought. They were bigger than the rabbits I was used to from Tennessee. Their heads were huge. Their ears were somewhat longer and much straighter. They looked sinewy and stringent. Elongated rabbits.

"Jackrabbits," Mrs. Svoboda said, pointing at the picture in my hand. She was smug about it, or maybe proud to know something that I could not possibly know. "Ezekiel and his father joined the men on many rabbit roundups."

Not knowing what to say, but happy that I was not being treated like a harlot at that time, I said, "Ma'am?" She had a stack of pictures of dead bunnies.

"Millions of jackrabbits came with the Dust Bowl," Ezzy said. "Not only couldn't we breathe air without dust or chew food without grit—"

"It was in our beds, our hair, our unmentionables," Mrs. Svoboda said. "Dust was everywhere. Constantly had to wash it out of your eyes. Nothing tasted good. You were always spitting out mud. Clouds of it came from nowhere. We thought it was the Second Coming."

"Right," Ezzy continued, trying to gloss over the apocalypse reference, "but there were thousands of rabbits eating what little crops we had growing. 'Hoover hogs,' we called them."

"We had to kill them."

"It was kill them or be killed. Like hogs, they ate everything in their path."

"No guns allowed during the roundups," Mrs. Svoboda said. "You could shoot them squarely, though, if there weren't no roundup. Peter shot a few one day when he was out in the field, trying to tend the few bits of wheat we had. Damn Hoover hogs couldn't care less what you and your kids had to eat."

"Peter was my father. We clubbed those rabbits with baseball bats, hammers, broomsticks, or ax handles. We weren't allowed to use guns for fear of killing someone else instead of a damned rabbit."

"Ezzy killed, I think, fourteen rabbits that day. Peter must have killed thirty-two. Or thirty-three. I can't remember. So many days of rabbit roundups. We held them on Sundays. They were events."

I looked at Ezzy and couldn't imagine it. Not even as a young farm boy with nothing to eat, I couldn't see him running around with a club, beating rabbits to death. Mrs. Svoboda placed the other pictures on the table and began eating her food again. I set the picture I had in my hand down and picked up another one. There were rabbits piled atop one another in a fenced-in area. Four very proud-looking farmers stood nearby. "What did you do with all those rabbits?" I asked. "Did you eat them?"

"No, we did not," Mrs. Svoboda said. "They had the rabbit fever."

"Tularemia," Ezzy said. "It can get you really sick. Or kill you, but that's kind of rare. So the men who rounded up those rabbit bodies wore some protection. Some people, though, ate the rabbits anyway. They're probably crazy today, or at least they're all scarred up. That is, if there was tularemia."

"Judge not, that ye be not judged," Mrs. Svoboda said. "But yes, I imagine so."

I shivered. What kind of person beats a rabbit to death? I knew the circumstances, but doesn't killing something so helpless compromise one's sleep? I suppose everything about the Depression did then, if you lived in the thick of it as Ezzy did. But those rabbits especially, lined up proudly with their bodies unnaturally stretched out. I wasn't able to eat anything else after talking about the jackrabbits, but at least we were all talking. And I was not being insulted by Mrs. Svoboda with her implications and coldness.

There was another picture. This one was of a woman, a farm wife, maybe, with coveralls on and her hair in a bun. Next to her was a young boy with a crutch. Unlike the woman, he was smiling. I picked the picture up and looked at it closer. Though it was in black and white, I could see that the world was pallid around them. I could see that they, too, were part of the Depression. "Is this part of your family?" I asked. I looked up at Mrs. Svoboda and thought I saw her face soften.

"Those were friends," she said. "The boy all grown up and not doing very well. But she's just as strong now as she was then."

"You still keep in touch with them?" Ezzy asked.

Mrs. Svoboda's face hardened again. "I check up on her," she said. "I think that is about all I can do for them."

Ezzy sucked his teeth. "He's using the crutch because of an accident with a jackrabbit roundup. That ain't his mother. That's his sister. His mother went crazy."

"Who the hell wasn't crazy after those years, Ezekiel?" His mother slammed her hand on the table. I looked away from the two of them. I looked out the window and saw how dark the night was, how the only light came from the room in which we sat.

Sometime in the middle of the night, Mrs. Svoboda turned.

I slept beside her on an old mattress that felt as if it were filled with hay. It was permanently indented in the middle. We went to bed once dinner was done, and after lying there for over an hour trying to fall asleep, I had gravitated toward Ezzy's large mother. I nuzzled up against her whether I liked it or not. I smelled her and felt her body rise with each difficult and assisted breath.

Her breathing at first disturbed me, but soon the rasping was rhythmic and lulled me to sleep. Much later, after I was well asleep, she turned. I was too tired to look at the clock, and the machine to which she was hooked up that helped her breathe shifted. She was quiet for ten, twenty, then thirty seconds. I could hear nothing but my blood—I held my own breath waiting for her rasp. I did not want to have come hundreds of miles to have some old lady die next to me. So I lay there, too scared to give her a shake, waiting for that rasp to continue, for that machine to hum as it was just seconds before.

Then it came.

Her returned breathing was stoic somehow. It was also reassuring and maternal. I felt safe when it came back. I let my eyes close and I listened to her, to the crickets outdoors, to the blowing prairie wind. These sounds made up what I could call a Kansas quiet, which actually was pretty noisy.

I was tired in earnest and knew I could fall asleep again. Still, in that peacefulness created by Mrs. Svoboda's heavy breathing, I opened my eyes again to verify my surroundings—that I was really there, beneath an ancient summer quilt, next to a large, strange woman—and saw how present the moon and the stars were out there in the middle of nowhere. In that darkness, I could clearly see the dresser, the bed on which we lay, and Mrs. Svoboda. I reached out and placed my hand on her shoulder, which rose dramatically with each breath, and kept it there for a minute. My hand elevated with her shoulder when she breathed in and descended when she breathed out. I then let her go and turned over.

When I woke up the next morning, the Kansas sun spilled across the house, already relentlessly hot. Mrs. Svoboda was out of bed. I had migrated to the center, forcing the mattress down in the middle with my weight. I felt better than I thought I would; I was actually well rested. My shoulder ached a little from sleeping on such a soft bed, but it was a surprisingly tranquil night after I had come to terms with my situation. I felt I slept like I never have before. I was not tired at all. But I was still wary of Ezzy's mother, and I was worried overall about the trip yet. In the next room, I could hear her speaking quietly with Ezzy in the kitchen. Flatware scraped loudly across their dishes.

Ezzy and his mother talked like old friends. It was clear that they would never talk like that with me or with any other nonfamily member around. I tried listening, but I heard only parts of their conversation. Many of their phrases, including "dead now" or "left her husband," stuck out. I lay there, wondering what the proper protocol would be for waking up in a house where one shared the host's bed and the only bathtub was in the only bathroom, which was in the far corner of the kitchen. I was wearing only a T-shirt and panties, the outfit I had to sleep in to appear somewhat decent for Ezzy's mother.

I heard "lost her fourth baby."

I had to pee. I couldn't hold it any longer. My bladder swished audibly as I moved from my left side to my back, to my right side. I got up from the bed, went to my suitcase, and dug through its contents until I found a pair of shorts. I threw them on, not buttoning the top button because it would have been too much for my bladder. I wanted to take a quick glance in the mirror, but Mrs. Svoboda's room was lacking in this aspect. I tried to picture myself in my mind and decided I looked presentable enough, and then I left the protective shield of the bedroom, padded through the kitchen to the bathroom, and held my head high as I went. I knew Mrs. Svoboda's and Ezzy's eyes were on me as I went to the john. I nodded at them in what I hoped to be a friendly fashion and continued toward the bathroom.

I had the feeling that the indoor plumbing here was new. The bathroom was closet-sized, and not the good-sized closet. The tub and toilet were stained and neglected. The mirror on the medicine cabinet was slowly fading; the silver of the mirror was overrun with black splotches. It was completely utilitarian: you went in, did your business, and got out.

A towel and a bar of soap were laid out for me on the toilet, so I had to move them into the sink to go to the bathroom. There was no fan, so no white noise, which made me worry that Ezzy and Mrs. Svoboda would hear every bit of me. I placed the towel into the tub and turned the sink's tap on and then used the bathroom, hoping the running water would cover up the sound of my going. Finally, I peed, the release making me shiver, the urine too warm. I flushed the toilet and waited for the pipes to quiet before I started the bath.

There was a large jar nearly filled to the top with slivers of lye soap of varying white next to the bathtub. A gel formed throughout the jar from the soap. The sight of this made Mrs. Svoboda almost believable to me, more real and approachable than she appeared. I had never seen anything like someone saving soap and I didn't know what she'd do with it. I imagined her making new bars of soap out of the slivers, packing them all into a square mold. The job would be expectantly quiet. The irony of the messy soap remainders would not be lost on her; it was here when she was alone that her sense of humor came through.

I moved the towel back to the top of the toilet when it was quiet in the bathroom again. Before I started the water in the tub, I heard Mrs. Svoboda say in an uncharacteristically loud voice, "Had lost her."

My bath was lazy and long. I didn't mind soaking and taking my time because I was not looking forward to being on the road again in the heat. The full tub of steamy water and the tiles blocked out their actual words, but I heard the tones of Ezzy and his mother talking in the kitchen. Their voices were calm, and the rhythm of their talk played like a duet. They didn't interrupt each other, but knew naturally the other's cadences. It was amazing: even after all these years, their own mellow opera. Maybe I could return home and fall into an old pattern of life with my parents. The last conversation I had with them was one of confusion and accusations. My father told me that he loved me and raised me in spite of who I really was, and my mother told me that I should be grateful to him for accepting me. Even so, I felt a pang of longing for my own mother hearing Ezzy and Mrs. Svoboda talk.

They seemed interested in what each other had to say. They were comfortable together. Their voices were too relaxing from where I sat—or lay—in the bathtub. I let my lids fall once and held my eyes closed for about a minute. Then I tried to wake myself up, fearing the worst. I opened my eyes again and thought about rock music. I thought about scary movies, favorite jokes, and anything else to keep awake. But still I closed my eyes. This time, I saw the rows of jackrabbits. My mind supplied the farmers with their makeshift clubs, beating hungry rabbits with no mercy. Boys and men bared their teeth, some silent, some screaming war cries. It was not hard to see; even in the gray and ecru I imagined the world to be during that time of dust storms and starvation, the color of the blood was an incongruous red. At that point, my eyes opened wide and I would not shut them again.

I bathed vigorously and quickly, scrubbing my skin pink, and worked the bar of soap into enough of a lather to wash my hair twice. After getting out of the tub, draining the water, and drying off, I wondered how I'd get myself from the bathroom back to Mrs. Svoboda's room, where, with my lack of foresight, I had left my clothes for the day. She seemed so prudish, I was afraid that a quick jaunt from the bathroom to the bedroom in just a towel would give her a heart attack. I stood there looking at myself in the mirror. My hair looked as if a cat had cleaned it, matted from the fat of the lye soap. And I could see what Mrs. Svoboda meant by dark. It wasn't the first time that the hue of my skin drew comments. And my hair, which I had thinned and chemically straightened every two months.

Mother and Daddy never told me anything until it was very clear that I may be different. And that conversation brought me here. My mother lectured me about bloodlines versus drops of blood while I packed a bag. I knew the purity claims and concerns, from mulatto to quadroon, octoroon, and all the way down to sang-mêlé. I could have asked where I was on the spectrum, but I figured the less I knew the better. But it wasn't just the fear of blood tainted by the darker race; where I came from, the bluer the blood the better. There could be no mixing of races or classes.

I had my suspicions from how soon I was born after their wedding, but never about who my father was. The way they dealt with each other, my mother and father, was loving, sure, but there was the sense of responsibility to each other that I didn't see in other couples. They reminded me of royalty forced to marry. They were often cagey about how they fell in love and often dismissed it as their parents knew each other.

My questions bothered my parents through childhood, but by high school, I bombarded them. "But where do I get my curls from? How come I don't have blue eyes like you or Daddy? Why is my hair so dark and coarse? Whose nose do I have?" They never had answers, or dismissed it as great-greats or the Anglo-Saxon ancestry or the French side. I realized the bother of my questions when I started getting them from classmates, followed by accusations, taunts that I should be at the other school. My family didn't like a scandal, so I decided to leave.

"But where will you go?" my mother had asked me. And what had I said? I was so angry that I don't remember how I answered.

"Let's not worry about it now," I said to the mirror. As far as I knew, I was as American as any other girl, and America is full of darkness. Anyone can make what they wanted to of that.

From the other room, I could hear that Ezzy and Mrs. Svoboda were still talking. I listened to the notes of their voices. Soon I was able to discern words, and the name "Ruth" was repeated a few times. "Ruth was seventeen," Ezzy said. "Too young and too skinny to even carry a child," Mrs. Svoboda said. Then I heard other tones, softer. Someone said, "It was 1933," exasperated, and I could not tell if it was Ezzy or his mother. I realized then how much alike they were. "Buried him on a Friday," and that was Ezzy for sure.

"She'd gone mad," Mrs. Svoboda said. A chill went through me, leaving me cold. I shivered and goose bumps puckered all over my wet skin. I felt all of my nineteen years and not a minute older. Hell, I felt like a child, much younger than I was, and wanted to go home. I wanted to be on an Adirondack chair in a screened-in porch while sipping something forbidden. I wanted to not hear about burials on any day and women named Ruth who had gone crazy. And if this Ruth was any kin to Ezzy, wouldn't he lose it, too?

I was Ruth's age when I left home, finding a job in a small town slightly north. I was a waitress where no one cared about my background. And that's how I met Ezzy, on his way to somewhere else.

I dug through the medicine cabinet until I found a thin black plastic comb, the kind greasers used to carry in their back pockets. I rinsed it in the sink and worked the tiny, close teeth through the thick mess of my hair. I worked slowly, watching the teeth divide thick strands as I ran the comb through. It somewhat worked.

"You should go see," I heard Mrs. Svoboda say. She said something else, but her voice trailed off. I missed it. Ezzy didn't reply right away. I realized I was still standing in front of the mirror, the comb at the crown of my head, waiting for his reply. "Should go see," she had said. See what?

Then Ezzy said my name. "Sissily really doesn't go in for all this," and his voice was lost. I dragged the comb through, followed its descent with my eyes, and let it go slowly so it wouldn't rip my ends. "Ruth," he said. He laughed. "Ain't seen her in years." But didn't she lose it? Ezzy was right: I would not go in for all that.

My hair wasn't getting any better. I quickly made a French braid, re-rinsed the comb, and put it back in the medicine cabinet. I inhaled air, muggy from the bath and dusty from the prairie dirt, and channeled courage. Breathed out. I left the bathroom with my head up and just a towel on, carrying the clothes I slept in in a neat bundle. Ezzy and his mother stopped talking when they heard the bathroom door open. I didn't pay any mind, only went on my way to get dressed.

"Leaving tracks," Mrs. Svoboda said. "Floor's all wet with her feet."

I pretended to not hear her.

Back in the bedroom, I dressed slowly, trying to think of excuses to not go see this Ruth, whoever she was. I slowed down more when I found I couldn't make an excuse: I had nowhere to be, no one to see. It was only me and Ezzy, and he was the one leading us, making all the rules and all the stops. My jeans weren't fully on when I considered how, since I'd left my family, I was absolutely dependent on Ezzy. All my basic needs and everything else were in his hands. I traveled in his car and I stayed where he wanted me to stay. I slept where I was told, like in his mother's bed. I hadn't wanted to do that, but I had no argument. Sure, she was the one who didn't want Ezzy and me sharing a bed, but could we not have stayed at a hotel? Some nice country inn? My head began to hurt. I felt frustrated for being someone else's responsibility. I could have lain back down.

I told myself if we went to see Ruth, whoever she was, Ezzy would protect me. Then I felt sick again: I didn't want to be under Ezzy's protection. I had become a kept woman, or maybe something worse than that.

Since there was no mirror, I had to trust that my hair looked okay. But I wanted to be sure. I looked around the bedroom again. On top of her dresser there wasn't much. I quietly opened drawers and found stodgy, color-less clothes, much like what Mrs. Svoboda wore the day before and that morning. In the top drawer were her inti-mate things, as homely and modest as one could imagine. I also found a lock of wavy hair. A long brunette lock kept by a small velvet bow. With the hair was a photograph: a woman with a sloppy bun. The woman was broad in the shoulders and looked strong. She had a slight smile, and though the photo was black and white, I suspected color in her cheeks. It was a picture of a woman who was being photographed by someone who loved her—that was clear to me. The air felt thinner around me; I couldn't figure it out. "It's not my business," I said under my breath. I replaced the picture and lock of hair, then closed the drawer.

I stood there unsure what to do next. No mirror, that's for sure. Why would Mrs. Svoboda ever have to look at herself? And as I stood there, I realized the woman was in the picture I saw at dinner. She was the sister to the little boy with crutches who got hurt in the rabbit round-up. Knowing this made me feel something else for Ezzy's mother, but I wasn't sure what. I already feared her, but maybe this was a different kind of fear. There was pity, too; if she loved this woman, she could have done nothing about it.

I shared a bed with her. I shuddered, afraid of my new knowledge. Did Ezzy know?

Mrs. Svoboda came in without knocking. Though I had my jeans on, I didn't have a top on yet. "What's taking so much time?" she asked. "You city women: up late, move slow. It's a wonder anything gets done there. And everyone is always talking about how fast it is in the city. I can't see how with women like you in it. Can you cook?"

"I'm from the South," I said. "We take it easy down there. And no, I can't cook." I quickly grabbed my T-shirt and pulled it on. "I mean that I don't know if I can cook or not. I never needed to cook."

"Needed, maybe not. What, you're fifteen? Sixteen? Your mama probably cooked for you all the time. But haven't you ever wanted to cook?"

"Our cook cooked. Sometimes, I made a sandwich, yeah, or leftovers. Have I ever wanted to cook? I guess I never thought about it. And I'm nineteen years old, Mrs. Svoboda. I'll be twenty next month. Mind if I sit down?"

"Do what you like."

I sat on the foot of the bed. "No, I guess. I can't cook, never wanted to cook. I don't like spending my time in the kitchen."

"Then how will you take care of Ezekiel?"

"What?"

"If you don't cook, how can you take care of my son? Keep house and cook for him? What I'm asking here, missy, is how can you run a home?"

I had never thought of it that way. Mrs. Svoboda's empty room became too small. I wanted to get on the road, away from Ezzy's mom and her self-assumed role of delegating responsibilities. I didn't want to "keep house," and I didn't think Ezzy wanted me to, either. "Women in my family hire other women to cook."

She asked, "Can you do me a favor, Sissily?"

I felt good about her using my name; I couldn't remember her ever having said it since we'd been there. I was still bothered by her, though. "What's that?"

"Convince Ezekiel to stop and visit Ruth. He ain't seen his sister in years, and I know she's kind of less than normal in the mind, but she's aware of her brother. She misses him and talks about him all the time."

"He has a sister?"

She looked as if I'd spat on her floor. "Yes, he has a sister. He has nephews and nieces older than you from

40

that sister. I had two other boys, but they died. One during the Depression, and one during the war. Didn't Ezekiel ever tell you about them?"

"I'll tell him," I said, ignoring her question, "but the car is his and he sits behind the wheel. I can't promise anything." I stood up and walked toward my bag. I wanted Mrs. Svoboda to stop talking and to stop telling me things that I wasn't supposed to know about. The Svobodas were inviting me in too much of their life, too much of their past. I feared adopting their midwestern attitudes and accepting their roots and views as the gold standard of perspectives.

"Hey, Sissily," she said.

I was beginning to be annoyed by her voice. I turned toward her and waited for the next ort of info that Ezzy would have kept from me until his deathbed, or for some other critical word regarding housework and house-wives. I feared that she'd tell me about the woman in the picture, or that she'd come on to me. What she did was try to pull me in more.

When she knew she had my full attention, she asked, "Will I ever see you again?"

I wanted so badly to say no and to be on the road again that I hurt for it. I had a craving for the windows being down, for the sun beaming boldly through Ezzy's Caddy's tinted windows and hurting my eyes in spite of my Wayfarer shades. I wanted it badly. But she had me there. Would Ezzy tell me anything on his deathbed? I might never really know him. I didn't want to tell her what I was thinking about, nor did I want to answer her question. "I don't know."

In front of the Svoboda homestead, Ezzy and I shared a long goodbye with his mother. Not much was said, really. Mrs. Svoboda once said, "I sure miss Darlene." Darlene was Ezzy's estranged wife. I shifted on my feet. "I sure would have liked to see her and Becky."

Ezzy said, "Well, we best be getting on the road. Think about what I offered to you, Mama."

"I like it here," she said. "I'm here with my husband and two boys buried out back. And I have my daughter and my grandbaby. Besides, if I go, who'd keep an eye out for Ruth?"

"She can come, too," Ezzy said.

"Naw, she can't. Neither one of us could go with you for obvious reasons. Besides, that young thing won't want your mama and sister around."

Ezzy slowly looked to me, his face tired and weathered. He looked at me as if he'd forgotten I stood there. *No, no,* I wanted to say. *Don't worry about me. I won't be there when Ezekiel comes around the next time.* But he reached his arm out to me. I flinched a little, but his arm kept coming. He grabbed me by my shoulder and pulled me closer. "Sissily is an understanding girl. She's kind and she's loyal. Hell, she slept in the same bed as you, so why would she mind if you come live with us? Mama, you don't even run the ranch anymore, save for a few bulls and heifers."

Mrs. Svoboda made a wet, defiant noise with her lips. It was a spell of silence before she said, "Well, don't be a stranger, Ezekiel," then she moved to him. He let go of me and went to her, went to be hugged like a good son. The embrace, again, seemed more business than love, or the business of love: firm, brief, neat. "Sissily," Mrs. Svoboda said. She reached out to me, almost reluctantly but very boldly, and I went to her, hugged her. It was brief, but I believe we were both sincere. At least I was. "Remember what I said about you all visiting Ruth," she said so quietly that Ezzy could not possibly have heard, but loud enough so it was not as intimate as a whisper. Then she let me go.

"It was wonderful to have met you," I said.

Then we were in the car. Ezzy hadn't started the engine yet; he only sat in the driver's seat, his head slightly lowered toward the steering wheel.

"You have a sister," I said.

"I have a sister. Ruth. Ruthy."

"We should go see her."

"You don't know anything about her."

The windows were still up, so it was close in the car. Already, I was sweating, and I wanted very badly to take my shirt off, but Mrs. Svoboda still stood outside and watched us. "Your mother is looking right at us. She isn't moving."

"I know," Ezzy said.

"Are you okay?" I put my hand on his back. He shrugged it off. "How far does Ruth live?" I asked. "If you don't want to go, that's fine. I can be done with meeting family for this trip."

He started the engine without a word. I sat back in my seat, still with my eyes on him.

"You want to meet Ruth?" he asked. He turned to me and looked as if he were going to tell me that there was no Santa Claus.

"Only if you do. Your mother suggested we see her. Hey, you wanted me to be nice to your family."

"No. I never wanted that. I just told you to behave, not take up any favors." Without looking at the road, Ezzy took off quickly. The Caddy's tires kicked up dirt, and rocks flew all around us. "Let's go see Ruthy and Mama's so-called grandbaby. It's just up the road. She's still on the ranch."

And just as quickly as he started, he stopped: he hit the brakes hard and made the tires squeal. His actions slammed me forward into the dashboard with too much force. I put my hands out to lessen the impact, but afterward my wrists and the heels of my palms were sore.

"We're here," he said. "See? Walking distance, really. Let's go." He then jumped out of the car and slammed the door behind him. I could hear him from inside of the car, calling for his sister. With his hands cupped around his mouth, he shouted, "Ruthy, come see your long-lost brother. Are you there? Are your babies there? Let's see you all."

I shuddered. The house was in much worse shape than the place we just left. Asbestos shingles from the roof were strewn about on the ground, as were car bumpers and other parts, well-worn clothes, food wrappers, tractor tires—anything one could think of was in Ruth's yard.

"Get out of the car, Sissily." Ezzy leaned down to the passenger-side window and looked in at me. He was still shouting. "We're here to see Ruth, my good sister. Come out so Ruthy can get a good look at you." He opened the door theatrically, bowed low, and held out his hand. "Chez Ruth."

"Ezzy, you're being silly."

"Am I? I heard you in there, talking to Mama. 'He sits behind the wheel,' you said. I thought we were doing this together."

"We are. That's not what I meant. I only wanted you to be able to see your sister and for you not to blame me later on if you missed her."

"Missed her? Sissily, I've been trying to miss her since I left Kansas. Before I left."

"Then why are we out here?"

"I don't know. Maybe so you can impress my mother."

"Isn't that what you wanted?"

He stood there, breathing at me angrily. "I don't know. I just wanted to see my mother. You just happened to be there."

"But what did you expect of me when we were there with her, if all you wanted to do was see her? 'Happened to be'? Was I supposed to be seen and not heard?"

Ezzy pursed his lips at me. "What is that supposed to mean?"

"What in the fuck do you think? What am I to you?"

He slammed the door hard. Unfortunately, my knee was sticking out a bit, so I got hit. I rubbed the mark, then flexed my knee. It hurt something awful, but I thought I was okay.

Outside, Ezzy kicked the tire and walked swiftly, but coolly, around to the driver's seat. I started panicking and didn't know what to expect when he got in. I could feel my heart beating as if I had run a mile. When he got to the door, he snatched it open and got in. He put the key in the ignition and started the engine. "She ain't here," he said. But we didn't move.

I caught movement behind him. Someone tall was coming. Taller than Ezzy, taller than his mother, taller than anyone I knew. "Ezzy, someone is there."

Quickly, the person came upon the car. I wanted to get away. The man was white like porcelain, his eyes pink, his hair the color of his skin, and, in his gaping mouth, his teeth few and separated. I could see the red of his tongue and his gums. From afar, I could hear what I took to be screaming, but soon I could recognize a word. A name. Ruth, whom we did not see yet, was calling this man's name. "My nephew," Ezzy said.

"Lazarus!" His name was Lazarus.

"I want to go, Ezzy," I said.

He breathed out long, slow. "We're here now, Sissily. They know we're here."

Lazarus had bent at the waist and was now staring into Ezzy's window, looking at us. "He's just an albino."

"A what?"

"No skin pigmentation. You and me, we have pigment. You have a little more than I got. He's like a white rabbit. He's just a rabbit himself: soft and slow. Slow in the head, though. That has nothing to do with his pigmentation. Look, Sissily, he won't hurt you." Ezzy made his breathing slow down again. "You don't have to worry about Laz." He hit his window. "Back up, Laz!"

The tall ghost-white man backed away from the car. Ezzy opened the door. "I'm your uncle Ezekiel. Where is your mother, Laz?"

"I'm here, Ezekiel." There stood Ruth, holding a shotgun. She had it pointed toward us. Toward Ezzy.

"Now, Ruth. You looking good." She was not. Her hair was long and brown with streaks of gray and sticks and burrs buried in it. Some of her hair was matted in rough, knotted braids. Her dress was just as I imagined it, and I realized only then that I had thought how Ruth would look, a woman who "had lost it." A woman who had children too young at a time when children were hard to be had or to survive.

"How come you here, Zeke? You trying to claim this property?"

"No, Ruth, I'm not. I have no interest in living in Kansas."

"Who's that in your car?"

Ezzy turned to me and looked. He winked at me. "My daughter," he said. "I brought her along to see Mama and you."

His daughter.

"And you don't want the land?"

"No interest at all. Put down that gun, Ruth."

Ruth lowered her gun. She walked a little closer and stopped. "Get on over here, Lazarus. My word, children like these." She stopped and tried to blow and shake the hair out of her face. "These kids. You all want something to eat?"

"No. We're just stopping through." Ezzy held up his hands and showed Ruth his palms. He got out of the car and moved a little away from it. Then everyone went quiet. Ruth, Ezzy, and Lazarus. The three stood almost equidistant from one another.

Inside the car, I sweated like a pig in a Tennessee smokehouse. I had to get out. When I did, making noise with the door and with feet against the sandy dirt, the three looked at me.

"Hi," I said.

"Daughter," Ruth said.

"This here's Sissily. She's"—Ezzy cleared his throat—"she ain't my daughter, Ruthy."

"Ruthy," Lazarus said.

"If she ain't your daughter, why you got her in your car?" Ruth asked.

"Sissily is a friend."

"Why are you here, Ez? If it ain't for the property, why you come around here after all these years?"

"To say hello. Just passing through."

"Passing," Lazarus said, his voice syrupy thick and deep. He went to Ezzy and took him in his arms. The word *enveloped* came to mind. He hugged Ezzy's head and neck. With his mouth still open, he kissed the top of Ezzy's head and left the hair wet. "Uncle," he said. Ezzy nodded.

"Get on away from there, Lazarus. Come by your mommy."

Lazarus let Ezzy go. He walked toward his mother. Slowly, Ruth lowered her gun. "Hello, Zeke. You said hello. Now go on. Wait! Do you have something for me?"

"What do you mean?"

"Money. Wait, did Mama send you out this way?"

"Sort of."

"Your friend," she said. She looked at me. Cautiously, she came closer. "Kind of a young friend." Her gun barrel was still down.

"She's a good friend. A good woman, Ruth."

She looked at me and got an impish grin on her face. "We were this young, and things were all fucked up," she said. She kept walking toward me. I stayed still, not sure how to move. "We were this young, strange men touched you so that you may eat, and your period stops coming, and you have a baby white as the moon. His little white head and pink eyes sucking at your beige breast and healthy brown nipples. As healthy a nipple as starvation would give you."

She was right in front of me. She wouldn't look away and I couldn't look away. "What color would you say I was then, Ezekiel? Peach? Brown? Beige? The sun has tanned me the color of cedar now. Rough as rawhide. The sun does that." She touched my face. "Watch that, little one," she said, her hand still on my cheek. "Watch that you take care of your pretty, peach-fuzzy skin. But you won't have a snow-white baby, no. Your skin's too dark for that. Ezzy, is she part Negro? Mexican, maybe?"

"We should go, Ruth," Ezzy said.

"Yes," I said. I nodded my head up and down. My hair flew around my head, around Ruth's hand on my cheek, her arm that was really, as she said, cedar colored, spotted with browner freckles all over. Skinny arm, but defined by years of lifting something. She let go of my face and grabbed my hair. She held a handful in her hand, not letting go.

"Pretty peach fuzziness all about you. But look, I'm dark as the sun would have me; you're darker yet."

"Ruth," Ezzy said. He touched the hand that held my hair. She looked at him. I saw a look of confusion in her face, as if she didn't know what was happening.

"Lazarus," she screamed over her shoulder. "Where are you, baby?"

"Ruth, let the girl's hair go."

She smiled so that she showed me all her remaining teeth, then let go of my hair.

"I need money, Ezekiel."

Ezzy reached into his wallet and brought out a few bills for his sister. "You're doing okay," he said to her. "It's not so bad here." Louder, he said, "Goodbye, Lazarus." He waved. The large pale-white man waved back. I waved, too, then jumped into the car. Ezzy was in soon after me, and he put the key in the ignition and started the engine. He put the car in drive and stomped his foot down on the accelerator pedal, trying to get that Cadillac up to sixty-five miles an hour as fast as possible.

In spite of our earlier argument, I was happy to be on the road again with Ezzy. Ruth was the scariest person I'd ever met, and I was glad to be away from her. In the car, we had the front windows cracked open and the back ones all the way down. I had my hand on his thigh and was just beginning to feel better about being on our way out of Seward County. We were quiet. Some music played softly on the radio. Lane lines and grain fields as far as the eye could see. I let my eyes close and leaned my head back on the headrest. *California, here I come.*

Then I had a thought that made me open my eyes and completely wake up: Could I see living with Ezzy for the rest of my life? My heart rate was starting to climb again. I wanted to look at him, but I didn't want to for fear of blurting out what I was thinking. I asked myself that question again, as I sat there with my heart beating ever faster, and I realized I had a lot of questions about California, Ezzy, and me. I tried to calm down, but then I remembered Ezzy's parting words to his mother before we left. I wanted to ask him how old Mrs. Svoboda was. Would she actually come live with Ezzy and me, and what would that entail, Ezzy and me living together? I assumed that being lovers was a lot different from being married. I guessed that marriage would involve running a house. Running a house would mean that the rooms were kept clean, the linens were fresh, the yards were maintained, and the kitchen was stocked. Ezzy had enough to hire a lady, but would he hire a lady if he had a wife? And being a wife may mean being a mother. I saw myself pregnant, like a cartoonist's exaggeration; I staggered across my mind's page with a round belly and my regular thin arms and legs.

But he hadn't asked to marry me.

I looked over at Ezzy. How old was he? Frank Sinatra's "Summer Wind," an almost too perfect song for the prairie, started to play on the radio. "Hey, Ezzy, what's going on, huh?"

Ezzy asked, "What do you mean?"

"I mean, do you want to marry me or something? Are you taking me to California for good, or for a fling?"

Ezzy took some time to answer. Of course, how was he supposed to answer that question? Not even I knew I was going to ask it, especially after what just happened at Ruth's, so it would have been better for me to leave that conversation for another day when we were easier with each other. While waiting for him to answer me—or to not answer—I listened to Sinatra sing.

"What do you think he means by 'piper man'?" I asked.

Ezzy turned the radio off. "Now do you want to know about this piper man, or do you want to learn about our life in California?"

"I mean," I said, "our life. That sounds so determined. I mean, your mother is so alone out there." My tempo accelerated as I spoke, my register went quickly up an octave, and my volume made a crescendo. "I mean, supposedly she has your sister, Ruth, but clearly, Ruth isn't very stable. And you may be worried that your mother is getting too old to be alone. Who am I supposed to talk to out there in California, Ezzy? I know the Cimmarons, but they're only there in March through May or something. I know the Ted Robinson clan, but his daughter and I are not really on speaking terms. I know the Farwells, but only distantly because that family is distant, as my mother always says, in geography (Betsy's her sister), but I can't talk to them. I'm running away from them. Not them, exactly, but from family, right? And friends, right? Ezzy, am I running away?"

"No."

"Running away from home!" I giggled uncontrollably. "What a grown-up thing to do." My head felt stuffy as if it were full of flu. My ears rang along with the wheels of the car driving down the country road. Through my giggling, I asked, "Do you want to be married to me? Am I expected to be a wife? To be pregnant? Do I want to be pregnant? If I get pregnant, then I'd have kids. I'd have to raise them."

"Sissily."

"Then I'd have to pipe down and become my mother. Pipe down? Piper. At nineteen, I'll be my mother. No more soirées in the Carolinas. No more escapades to Atlanta. No more jaunts up north to New England, and no more meeting men like you. No more meeting men! Instead, I'll go to Tupperware parties and teas with the League of Women Voters or the United Daughters of the Confederacy or whatever, because they may not have daughters there in California. Not that the Daughters would want me anyway. Not now."

"You're crying, Sissily."

I wiped at my face with the backs of my hands. I was crying. And I was blabbering on about my life ending. But I was laughing, too, and it dawned on me that I was hysterical. It was so feminine, so typically woman, it disgusted me, which made me cry more and laugh more. "I don't want this! I don't want it at all!" And I was yelling, too. Snot started dripping out of my nose, and my throat was hurting from sobbing and yelling.

Ezzy looked quickly at me and then back at the road. He rushed the car onto the shoulder, decelerating quickly as we went. Gravel pinged off the car's undercarriage and the wheels burned rubber a bit as Ezzy forced the car to a quick stop. He jumped out of the car and ran around the front of the Brougham Special, but slowly enough so that I could make out that he was upset. He looked dangerous. Frightened, I slid across the front seat to the driver's door. I let myself out and ran across the road, into a wheat field. Still crying and laughing and now hiccupping, I trampled the tall grain and thought that I was getting away. I looked behind me quickly to see that Ezzy was not so far behind, but there was enough distance between us to make me feel somewhat comfortable. I kept running and left the field of wheat and jumped to an adjacent lot, much smaller, full of lacy white wildflowers and orange flowers. I was slowing down—I felt as if I had just run miles. My ankles itched and burned from nettles.

I heard Ezzy behind me, his footsteps louder. His was in a relentless and steady pursuit. I looked behind me again, briefly, and saw that Ezzy's hand had disappeared in the fabric of his shirt. I remembered the gun and became more afraid. Adrenaline allowed me to pick up speed, but I stopped abruptly when I heard it go off, and then I covered my ears in the useless silence that followed the gunshot. Or I stopped when I saw the jackrabbit, hopping unnaturally high in the air, slightly right, his head cocked and his ears skewed. I want to say that I saw blood flying, but that couldn't be true. Maybe seeing the rabbit made me stop, then hearing the gun. However it happened, soon Ezzy grabbed me, wrapped one arm around my neck, and held the still warm gun to my head. "Don't you ever leave me," he said.

After he tried to round me up in the middle of Kansas, Ezzy woke up and made love to me, never asking me if he could. It was not exactly making love, just him sweating on top of me, whispering nothing, only grunting when he neared orgasm. He pulled out before finishing without a word, pulled away from me, turned away from me. He went back to sleep, and I lay there in the hotel bed, in pain and afraid. I got up to go to the bathroom and wash up. Surprisingly, I found that I was bleeding. And I was very sore. I ran a warm bath and filled it with bubbles. Got in. I sat there until the water grew tepid, stayed in the tub to empty and refill it, then sat there until the water cooled again. I drained the tub. Refilled it. I thought seriously about finding my way back home or to somewhere else.

In the morning, Ezzy woke me up. My head was resting on the tiled wall and one hand was floating in the water and one outside the tub. "Trying to kill yourself?" he asked. I only looked at him. I got out and got dressed. My puckered skin took what seemed like hours to get back to normal.

As he packed, he didn't speak. He packed for both of us. I watched him, unsure what was going to happen next. We had a ways to go yet; now, we were on the edge of Kansas. We didn't make good time the day before. I sat on the edge of the bed. Ezzy kept working. And when he finished, he left the hotel room, not saying a word to me. I followed him out, not knowing what else to do.

In his car, he lit a cigarette and took a few drags before leaving the parking lot. I wanted a cigarette, too, but I couldn't bring myself to ask. Before entering traffic, he finally spoke. "Hungry?"

"Yes," I said.

"We can get something to eat. It'll take us another two days or so on the road. Are you okay?"

"Okay?"

"What had happened . . ." He stopped. He pulled out and followed the road into town. It was a small, forgettable frontier town that was more ghost than people. We found a diner off the main strip for breakfast. Inside of the restaurant, I noticed that it was ten degrees hotter in that dining room, which smelled of bacon and old grease.

"I guess we seat ourselves," Ezzy said. He grabbed one of my elbows and led me to a booth. These were left over from the 1940s, maybe the '50s, Naugahyde covered, foam filled, and scratched up by years of behinds. The waitress was quick in getting our order because we were the only patrons there besides an ancient couple having oatmeal and coffee at the counter. When the waitress took Ezzy's order, she said, "And what would Dad be having today?" I looked out the window and listened for Ezzy to correct her, but he didn't. He only ordered.

The waitress left us alone.

"Ezzy, what were you going to say?" I said.

He laughed a little. "If I didn't say it, it wasn't important."

"Before we left the hotel?"

"I don't remember me starting to say anything."

The waitress came back with our coffees and cream, then left again. I fixed my cup the way I liked it and took a long sip. "Nice," I said.

Ezzy took his coffee black. He took a short taste and nodded. "We will run out of things to talk about. I'll run out of things to say."

"Will you leave me here?"

"What kind of man would that make me, Sissily?"

"I guess you're right." I couldn't get situated in the booth. One side was higher than the other, and more than one spring sprung back for the last time ages before I got there. "If you're afraid of that," I said, "then why would you take me with you?"

Ezzy sighed long and heavy. The action looked like it depleted him. He reached for a cigarette in his shirt pocket and took out a nearly empty pack. He shook the last two cigarettes out and lit them and gave one to me. "I don't know why I put that gun to your head. I guess I should apologize. I was kind of crazy-headed. My mother"—he paused, drawing from his cigarette again, and flicked the ash into the tin ashtray on the table—"makes me that way. My sister, too. I don't know what to say to that. Sorry you had to see it, is all."

I reached across the booth and rubbed his knuckles. I squeezed his hands, then let go. I blamed his mother, too; she had put something untoward into our trip, even with her friendly goodbye. It was because of her that we stopped at Ezzy's sister's place, but I wasn't going to tell him I felt that way about his mother. "I didn't know jackrabbits were so big," I said. "I didn't realize they made a sound. I thought all rabbits were quiet."

"Unless you kill them. Jackrabbits make a lot of sound when they're in pain."

"It was like a baby crying. It was horrible. Hey, Ezzy, I can't believe you killed all those jackrabbits. That you killed anything, huh? I never had to do that, you know? Never had to kill a thing." I shivered. "I can't imagine handling a gun."

"We should teach you how to shoot."

"That's one thing I don't want to learn. I'm from the South, but I'm from the city. You know, Memphis is civilized." I noticed a long ash building on my cigarette. I wasn't smoking it at all. I took a puff and it was dead—the fire went out. I stubbed it anyway. "I don't think I'm ready for all of this, Ezzy."

I spoke without thinking, but after I said it, I bemoaned my rash behavior. Not the first time I got in trouble for my smart mouth, and certainly not the first time I got in trouble with Ezzy because of something I said. His gun wasn't too far from his hand; he could have grabbed it and shot me there in that booth, at that diner. Instead, he drew in air. Breathing in straightened his back out and displayed his muscles. When he spoke again, he sounded very placid and somewhat guilty.

"I know," he said. "I don't think you're ready for this, either. I don't want to cage you, Sissily. And I don't want to be an all or none man. You have to stop depending on me." He shook his head as if in shame.

"You know what I thought back there? I thought that I was hysterical. I'm in your car, going through it and thinking it. I'm hysterical. Can you believe it? That gun to my head was like being slapped. That gun to my head may be what I needed."

Ezzy leaned closer to me and let his face relax into a goofy grin. It made him look younger, more like someone my age than like my father's. But he said, "You don't know what you're talking about," and I saw an old man again. An authority figure.

The waitress came with our breakfast and left us to eat. We fell into silence again. I ate my eggs with the hope that I wouldn't associate the taste of over easy eggs with fatigue and worry. How far was it to the nearest depot? Would Ezzy take me there? I could go to New York. My mother told me if I wanted to look, I could find my real father there. The man who didn't raise me. The man who couldn't raise me. She told me this quickly, when I was all packed and dragging my bag. My father was on his way up the stairs. She whispered, "I know where he is. He writes sometimes and I write him. You could meet your other father." And that was it.

In that booth, I held back tears I had. I couldn't know it then, but I was grieving the self that was leaving me. I was losing who I thought I was for too long. I looked at Ezzy to gauge his mood, but I couldn't tell anything. All I saw was a middle-aged man who was no longer appealing. He opened his mouth as if to speak, but he shook the words away with a jerk of his head and stuffed his mouth with whatever meat he was eating. We were done talking.

PART 2
1947

Everyone wore cowboy hats in Kansas. That's what I first noticed when my family arrived in 1947. The hats and that men's legs were bowed open like wishbones. At first I felt so far outside of Wisconsin that I ached. Like a phantom limb, I'd feel a breeze that felt like it blew over Lake Michigan before reaching me, and when I turned to meet it, I'd realize that was no water, just dry plains.

The second thing I noticed was Lucky. But only after he noticed me. We were still new to Liberty, Kansas, when my family's car broke down. We found ourselves near Lucky's garage and were thankful that he served black customers. When our Chevy Deluxe sedan, coughing smoke and knocking, rolled into his garage, Lucky rolled out to meet us in his wheelchair, a Victorian contraption with a wicker back. The thing had wooden wheels with wooden dowels for spokes. My father cut the engine and got out of the car and introduced himself to Lucky. My mother got out, too, as if she wanted to give my father support. For a while, I stayed in my seat, but I got bored so I got out. Daddy shot me a look, but I ignored him.

While the three of them spoke (really, just the two of them, since Mama wasn't saying much), I took a self-guided tour of Lucky's garage. I picked up hand tools and tried to figure out their function; I handled car parts if I could. Somehow, Lucky moved away from my parents, or maybe I moved closer to him. My parents were talking over whatever needed to be done with the car. Lucky stood slightly out of his chair, leaned closer to me, and quietly said, "You have the most beautiful eyes I've ever seen." Then he sat back down and wheeled toward my parents, leaving me confused. I couldn't believe a white man really gave me a compliment and wondered if I should tell Daddy.

"Yep, the only thing I figure is the radiator, Mr. Johnson," Lucky said. "I don't have a hose here. I can order one in, which could take a few days, or maybe you and I can ride on down to the junkyard to see if they don't have an old Deluxe there with its radiator hose intact."

"We don't have time to wait," my father said. "We live there in Kismet. We've got to kind of have it today."

"Let's go on down to the junkyard, then. We can take my truck." My father hesitated, but then followed Lucky as he wheeled to an old pickup truck. My father stood next to the tailgate and waited patiently. Lucky was by the passenger door, unaware of my father's self-subordination, also patiently waiting. About a minute passed before my mother said, "David, I think the mechanic wants you to ride up front."

My father looked to Lucky to see if my mother had guessed right. Lucky nodded and motioned for my father to walk up to the cab. "We should be back soon, Raina," he said to my mother. "You two be fine in this garage?"

"We'll be fine," Mama said.

Lucky used his wheelchair as a brace for getting up on the kick board, then into the cab of the truck itself. I never understood why Lucky didn't have something more modern. He was slim but muscular—his forearms and hands were the product of pushing himself around in his chair, or working in the garage, or working on his family's farm. When Lucky did walk, his legs were terribly bowed, and the left one didn't move at all at the knee. You could tell, whether he sat or stood, how skinny his legs were, one more so than the other. They were like a child's legs on a man's body. His hair was dark brown and straight, his eyes blue, and his skin was the color of the reddish earth of Kismet. But I wouldn't know so much about how Lucky looked or about his farm until later.

Daddy, looking a little concerned, stepped easily up onto the kick board and into the truck. I imagined him fretting about riding next to a white man, a disabled white man at that. I was certain he thought about how Lucky got to be maimed, but he'd never ask, knowing such a question to be rude.

My mother and I were left sort of huddling in the garage. We watched them drive away, then we stood there with our arms folded over our chests. The wind was blowing hard and two actual tumbleweeds blew by. "Back home in Milwaukee," my mother said, "it would be time to plant the bulbs. Apples would be coming in and perfuming the backyards. Tomatoes would be up, too."

"When we were in Milwaukee," I said, "back home for you was Georgia."

She laughed. "David says I'll never be happy. Maybe that's so, but what's wrong with a little nostalgia? I know that Georgia won't be the same."

"But if we went back to Milwaukee, it'll be just as we left it. We ain't been gone that long."

"Nella, we'll do whatever we can to support your father. He is the one who makes sure we eat. I am a little wary of Kansas already—I keep expecting to see John Wayne walking by with a six-shooter in each hand."

"Milwaukee had way more trees. Out here, it's so flat it's like the land wouldn't even consider trees."

My mother laughed again, this time bumping into me playfully. We continued talking about what we missed about Milwaukee and what we hated about Kismet, and the whole time we spoke and waited, I wondered about what that white man said to me. This was before I knew his name. This was before I knew he was, really, still a boy, because all white males to me were men at that time.

Later at home, I obsessed over his words, worked them over in my head. Night and day, I replayed the incident in my mind whether I wanted to or not. It got to the point where I had to find out for sure if he'd actually commented on my eyes, so I hitched a ride toward Liberty a few days later.

A white woman picked me up. She was my parents' age or maybe a little older, it was hard to tell. I was unused to their skin, and hers was almost translucent, too many veins showing beneath it. So many colors were evident: purples and blues, greens, peaches, and pinks. There was as much the color white about her as there was the color black about me. But she looked undone. White people aged quickly, I was told, so this woman who demanded that I sit in back could be anywhere from forty to sixty for all I knew.

I got into the back of her car and she started talking right away. She took off, kind of quickly, and sucked her teeth loudly. I thought it'd be a silent trip, but she kept talking. "What you are doing is reckless," she said.

"Ma'am?"

"Hitchhiking. What if some wild boys picked you up? Raped you? I know that's the worst-case scenario and I'm always looking at the bad end of it, but it is a viable scenario." She turned toward me and looked at me too long to be paying attention to the road. Reflexively, my hand shot up and pointed toward the windshield, visually telling her to watch the road. She looked quickly ahead of her, but turned back around to face me. "Do you understand me?" she asked, swerving a bit while steering blindly.

"Yes, ma'am, I do." *Reckless.* It was, but I liked it. Then, without any prior thought or even knowing I'd do it, I lied: "It's the only way I can get my car back, ma'am."

"You mean over there by that crippled boy?" Her jowls were loose and shook a bit as she talked. "I only picked you up because you're a girl before you're colored. Men don't care what color it is. It's all the same to them. You know what *it* is I'm talking about. Hell, they may treat you worse with you being Negro and all. When they rape you."

She looked so other, I wanted to tell her to stop the car, to go back home and quit this chase. If anything was really said by that auto mechanic, then what of it? Could I actually touch a white person like that? Take him seriously as my boyfriend? He would be so foreign, too, that I didn't think I could. But curiosity got me, so I rode on, listening to the woman natter on about safety and sex-crazed men.

"Well, haven't I saved you?" she asked, pulling in hard on the side of the road. "You ought to be grateful."

"For the ride? I am grateful."

"Hitchhiking ain't smart. It's not safe. Thank the Lord that a good Christian woman picked you up. Thank the Lord for keeping you."

"I will."

"I would have driven you to the garage's front door, but it'd be unseemly, a white woman chauffeuring a black gal around."

"This is fine, ma'am. I could use the walk."

She pursed her lips and turned away from me, facing the road again. I thanked her once more, thinking that the walk would give me time to collect my thoughts and myself before facing Lucky. When I got out of the car, I walked a pace away, turned, and looked at my white lady chauffeur in her aging Packard, watched her as she drove away. *I should just walk toward home,* I told myself. *Leave this fool's errand for fantasy and speculation.* But I turned on my heel and walked toward the garage.

My oxfords were soon covered with the copper Kansas dirt, as was the hem of my dress. Although deep in thought, I tried not to look down but around me. I had looking down as a bad habit, and whenever I looked at the ground, I would find myself feeling low, too, thinking low thoughts. So I made myself look at the clear late July sky, at the wild grasses that grew along the footpath, yellowing in the season, and at the towering sunflowers looming to the left of me. It was a scene right out of a Laura Ingalls Wilder book. And it felt as peaceful as that, somewhat, but there was something underlying, something not quite right. That sense of unease was more out of *The Wizard of Oz* than Wilder: witches hiding and watching and waiting. I looked toward those aging sunflowers and a shiver ran over me.

I walked faster toward the garage. Then I stopped when I thought about what this mechanic was capable of. I'd heard the stories. I knew white men often molested colored girls and got away with their crimes. Was he liable to hurt me like that? As I thought through this, my steps slowed and I kicked up less dust. Soon, I was on a gravel walk. I considered Lucky's condition—he was in a wheelchair, I told myself. He could walk, I argued. I'd seen him stand up and move. But his walking was slow. I could run away if he tried anything. But where to? For how long until someone picked me up?

It won't happen, I told myself. *He is not that type of man,* I rationalized, not really knowing any type of man back then. I picked up my speed again and walked faster toward the garage.

The building looked different walking up to it instead of driving up to it, seeing it from the back seat through clouds of cigarette smoke. It was a very neat place: grasses and bushes trimmed to respectable heights, paint kept up, the dirt walk swept. A large red-and-white sign that read LUCKY'S GARAGE was tacked proudly above the garage doors. I didn't see him right away, so I walked into the building. Still not seeing him, I walked farther inside, passing a car that was being serviced. I heard him before seeing him. I walked a little slower, softer, and there he was. Lucky was working in the back, softly polishing a chrome bumper on a vehicle. He had no idea I was there. I felt silly and did not know my next move. I stood there in my fear and uncertainty and watched him make soft circles with the white paste on that bumper. Something in me moved me to speak. Maybe it was just the desire to move, to not stand there all day staring at this man.

"You said my eyes were beautiful." I tried to make my voice match Billie Holiday's— songlike even in conversation. But he didn't hear me over his radio. He was listening to some detective show. Much less sexy, but good and loud, I said it again. He turned slowly and stared me up and down.

"Your Chevy didn't break down again, did it?" he asked. He smiled like a salesman. He rolled away from the bumper and toward me.

"Chevy ain't here," I said, my voice much quieter, more like a girl's than a sex symbol's.

He stopped at his desk and, with effort and the support of his chair, stood up. "Please, have a seat." He motioned at the chair placed in front of him. "Are you with your parents?"

"I came alone," I said. I walked toward him and tried my best to talk slower because I had the tendency to talk too fast. I felt the switch in my hips I learned from my girlfriends back home, the switch that came automatically when you walked heel-toe to heel-toe. I made it to him, but I didn't sit down.

Lucky sat down again, hard on his behind, as if he wasn't sure of his place. "Alone." He laughed a little, more to himself than to me. "Yes, I did say your eyes were beautiful."

Not sure what I should do next, I stood in front of him, looked down at him. "What did you mean by that? Was that a . . ." But I didn't know what else to say.

"I meant that your lashes are long and dark. They frame your brown eyes. Your eyes are big like, I don't know, like the moon would be too clichéd."

"Then like what?"

"Like nothing else I've ever seen. I didn't say your eyes were beautiful. Not just that. I said that they were the most beautiful eyes I've ever seen. There is a difference."

The environment of the garage started to get to me. The smell of oil, gasoline, and grease made me woozy. I stepped back a little toward the door I came in. Lucky wheeled in closer to me. "You've come all that way, alone, to find out what I said about your eyes?"

I backed away a bit more. "I don't know," I said. "I'm sure I want to know more."

"Such as?"

"Such as how dare you compliment a black girl in that way?"

"Black? Is that what it is today? I thought it was Negro."

"Don't tell me what my race is."

"I thought you had to know about your eyes. I kept thinking about them, since that day." He wheeled in closer yet, and I backed up only one step. "I wondered how I could find you in Kismet. Are you from there? There ain't many of your kind there."

"My kind? You talk like I'm an animal or something."

"Now, nah, I didn't say that. I didn't mean it that way." He stopped and looked toward the ceiling. "I think I've only seen three black people besides you and your folks in my entire life. One was a traveling preacher who visited our church for some reason. He gave a sermon. It was kind of heated. All fire and damnation, was that guy. The other time, a young couple came in when their car broke down a couple of miles away. They were really afraid of me. It was the first time I've ever known someone to be afraid of me. I couldn't put a digit on the way they treated me—heads down, voices soft—until they had already gone. Their car fixed, of course. That's what I do."

"You talk a lot," I said.

"I like to talk."

"Do you like people being afraid of you?"

"Nah, I don't. It makes me feel, I don't know, uncomfortable is the best way to put it, I suppose. I tell you, it made me feel as scared as they were. They acted as if something was wrong with the situation, and I just followed suit. You know, they were the customers, and the customers are always in control. You acted that way at first, you and your mother. I didn't want to encourage it. But I saw a flash of your eyes." He stopped talking. He looked at me and I looked right back. "I had to tell you about them. After I told you, I saw you staring me down when you and your parents were here. I was afraid that I was too forward."

"There you go with fear again. You kind of did say something too forward, but it wasn't that."

"Well, what was it then?"

I shrugged. "Here we are talking, and I haven't told you my name. I am Nella." I held out my hand. He took it in his but did not shake it. "And what is your name?" I asked.

"It's writ large all over this garage."

"Lucky? That's your real name?"

He laughed. "You want to go for a walk? I can tell you then. I can push myself or you could push me." He let go of my hand.

"I can push. Just tell me where."

"First, let's just go out the door."

I made my way around to the back of him and grabbed the handles of the chair. It was smooth going until we left the garage. The dirt and rocks made the pushing difficult. I pushed at an easy pace at first but found I was getting no traction, so still holding on to the handles, I shoved the wheelchair hard. We went forward.

"Just go toward the road for a little while. Then you'll see a walking path jutting left. Take that path," he said.

It was somewhat disconcerting to hear him talking and to know that I was being talked to, but to not be able to see his face because he sat in front of me. I couldn't read him, looking at the back of his head that way. And being nervous didn't help. Plus pushing him was exercise. We walked in silence on the gravel pathway, and I thought about how difficult it would be to hear him go on as he liked to do with the noise the chair made on our trip. It didn't help that the wheelchair was so old. I was afraid that the thing was going to fall apart—it was a wonder that it was still together.

We had yet to make it to the walking path, but I was wiped out. I stopped to catch my breath. "Would you rather I push?" he asked.

"Does it get easier?"

"It always does. Eventually, it'll get easy for you, too. But not today. Let me push, then you can walk beside me."

"Okay." Walking next to him was strange, too; you always expect someone your age or older to be closer to you in height. Lucky rode about a foot beneath me. It all seemed too much—his race, his being in a wheelchair, his being so out of the way from town.

"You'll get used to this," he said.

"You say that as if I'm coming back."

"You are. Or I'm going to go see you. Or we'll meet in between."

"How are you so sure, Lucky?"

"You know, Lucky's fine. I'm okay with you calling me that. If you prefer, you could call me Janus."

"Isn't that a woman's name?"

"Hey!" He laughed. "No, not a—well, I guess it can be considered one. I never thought about it. My parents were German. It's a German name. Janus Obeck. It's my father's name, but I stopped calling myself a junior when he died. And I was called Janus until I was eleven. My sister, Greta, broke my leg in a few places. Not on purpose, though."

"How did she do that?"

"Here. Turn left." He pointed by pushing his chair leftward. "I somehow got mixed up in a jackrabbit round-up. They used to gather all these rabbits and put them in pens. Club them. Somehow, I made it in the mix. I don't know, maybe following Greta around. Yep, that sounds like me. I followed her everywhere back then."

"Why did they round up rabbits?"

"They still do sometimes, but that year, I guess, was pretty bad for farmers and rabbits. Thousands of jackrabbits. They had to do something with them. Where are you from?"

"Milwaukee."

"That's a sizable city. No jackrabbit problems there, I suppose."

I laughed. "Not that I know of. She broke your leg into pieces?"

"Yes. And she's still bothered by it all. Then, two years later, I got polio. I survived it but lost the use of my other leg. The lame one just got worse. People said I survived the Devil twice. Started calling me Lucky. Lucky stuck—I liked it better than my dead dad's name. Plus, I felt lucky. Still do."

"How old are you now?"

"How old do I look?"

He stopped moving and looked up at me. I looked down at his face. Light laugh lines were in the corners of his eyes. Fair freckles dotted his cheeks, but you had to be close to see them. A faint blond beard was growing. His nose was very pointy. His lips were full, but narrower than anything I was used to. And, of course, he had that translucent skin similar to the woman who drove me to his garage. Granted, it was darkened by the sun, but I could still see the blues, the greens, and the reds of the veins right beneath it. I said, "I don't know."

I looked away from him. Staring at him like that was imposing. So instead, I looked up, or, really, straight ahead. "How long were we walking?"

"A little while."

Why hadn't I noticed the sun was setting? Why hadn't I noticed the noise of his chair competing with the noise the wind made through the leaves and petals of the towering sunflowers that surrounded us? We were walking a small path that was only wide enough for the two of us. To our right and left, rows of sunflowers shimmied like chorus dancers wearing too much fringe and sequins. Flowers never frightened me until that moment. I thought back to what the white woman told me on the way there: "They may treat you worse with you being Negro and all."

"Isn't this wonderful?" Lucky said.

I looked back down at him. He was no "they." He was only one white man. In a wheelchair. Doing that— looking down—I realized why I hadn't noticed my surroundings: I was not looking up at the sky or even straight ahead. Lucky engrossed me. "It's like out of *The Wizard of Oz*. The field of poppies or something."

"It sure is. I come out here—hey, you're getting that scared look in your eyes. You scared out here?"

"No. Not exactly. Should we walk back?"

"You are scared. Come here."

"No, let's go back now."

"Relax, Nella, come here."

"How do I do that? Do I bend down?"

"Yes. Or would you rather I get up?"

"Oh, no, I can bend down." I tried to squat so that we were face-to-face but felt afraid.

"What do you want this to be? Just the one trip out here, or is it going to be how I want it to be? Seeing you all the time?"

"Lucky, that is a ridiculous thought. I don't see that happening. How lucky could I be getting a ride out here like I did today?"

"Kiss me and tell me you can never see me again."

"Kiss you? I should have listened to that lady who drove me here."

"What lady? Who drove you here?" He looked worried. He even glanced over his shoulder.

"Does that concern you? Who saw me come here?"

"Nella, what lady?"

"I hitchhiked here."

"Hitchhiked? Really? That is very dangerous, Nella. You're lucky it was a woman who picked you up."

"Yeah, that's what she said. Lucky. Don't you hate sharing your name with a word that's used so often?"

"You get used to it just like anything else. How are we going to get you home?"

"Well, first we're going to walk back the way we came and get back out in the open."

"You're not hitching again. I'll give you a ride back. Partially. I don't want your father coming after me. And I don't know how the town . . ." and there, he trailed off. But soon, he was talking again. "We'll figure it out. Please, kiss me. Or let me kiss you. Let me kiss your cheek."

"Tell me how old you are first."

"Okay." I leaned in close to him and turned slightly so that he could have my ear. He came close and breathed in, smelling my skin. Then he kissed me lightly on the cheek and withdrew slowly. I closed my eyes the entire time and kept them closed for a little bit after, listening to the drying sunflowers sway swiftly in the wind.

We were in a large field near the edge of Lucky and his sister's property. To get there, I had to take a bus to the edge of town and walk just short of a mile. Lucky had to drive a couple of miles and he had the advantage of a car. When we had made our plans to meet that first, official time as Lucky and Nella, the courting couple, he expressed his worry of my having to hike such a distance, but I assured him that I was a big girl and could make it on my own.

I could see his truck from the bus before I got off, and I pictured him waiting patiently in the cab. But once off the bus and walking, I could see him sitting beside his tailgate in his chair. I walked across a lot overgrown with wild carrots. As I got nearer, I could see that Lucky held a woman's black fedora in his hands. He sat there looking smug, twirling the hat on his pointer finger, when I finally reached him. "You want me to ask about that hat, don't you?" I said.

"You need no prompts from me, apparently." He was still smug.

"Well, why do you have the fedora?"

"If you're going to play clandestine lover, you have to look the part."

I stood about a foot away from him. "You should antici-pate my asking if I'm only playing, then. Acting, or being?"

"No, actually I anticipated that you'd run to me and jump into my arms. Plant kisses all over my face."

"Nope, you ain't going to get that. I figure we need to do some proper courting, as my mother would say."

"Well, what do you expect? For us to go to a movie together? Maybe out to eat? To one of the local dances?"

"Don't be smart."

"How do I court—or would I court—a woman I'm not supposed to be seen with?"

"I don't know. Flowers, maybe? Candy?"

"I brought you to sunflowers. I bought a hat for you."

"Give me my hat." I snatched the fedora from Lucky and put it on, slanted it forward to hood my eyes. "Sneaky enough?"

"It is. It's becoming, too."

"Don't I know it. Let's go argue somewhere else."

"Is that what this is? Arguing?"

"We're not agreeing."

"Okay, then let's not argue. Should I carry you? You walked a mile, after all."

"A mile's not long to walk. Do you mean in your chair?"

"I do."

"Will you push me?"

"You'd sit on my lap."

"No. Really, Lucky, it's too soon. I was serious about that courtship. I think that kiss last time was too forward."

"Did you like it?"

"Can we walk and talk?"

"We're not going far. I brought something else besides the fedora." He lifted a blanket he had across his lap to show a basket. Why hadn't I noticed that? "Here's dinner. We'll eat at that next field over there. I think those are poppies growing there."

"You're a card. This is not Oz, man."

"Seriously, more carrot and some brown-eyed Susans, old crocuses. Lots of bees. Not afraid of bees, are you?"

"I ain't afraid of anything."

"But sunflowers."

I took my new hat off and hit him on the head. We then walked on, quietly, me with that same sensation as I had earlier when walking with Lucky—that we were off balance. I asked if he wanted me to push, but he said he was fine, that maybe he'd need a push later. I shrugged and walked, enjoying the weather, the smells of the untended outdoors, and the sounds of the wind, the birds, even the mosquitoes and other insects flying by my ears. We found our spot, and I took the blanket from Lucky and laid it out on the ground. We then both lay on the blanket with the basket between us. "I hope you like chicken salad. My sister made it."

I was impressed by the meal: chicken salad sandwiches, potato salad, pickles, apple pie, and bananas. All the food was prepared by Lucky's sister, Greta, who made all his meals. She would send him home with a week's worth of food every Sunday after their weekly brunch. He said I'd like her. I jokingly asked him if I would ever get to meet her, but he shrugged. "Greta's weird. It'll probably be that I introduce you to her and she won't even bat an eye. Won't take a second look, really. She would be more surprised that I had a girlfriend than of your being Negro."

"Black. Jesus, Lucky, I'm black."

"Sorry. Black. She's just not that interested in race matters."

"Haven't you had a girlfriend before?"

"Yes. A few."

"Serious girlfriends?"

We were eating our sandwiches while sitting a little distance from each other on the blanket. When we were both sitting down together, especially down on the ground, it felt natural talking to him. We were seeing each other eye to eye. I had to get that feeling when we walked together, when he was in his chair.

"Like, were you ever in love?"

"No. Well, I was going to ask this one girl to marry me."

"That right? What happened?"

"I don't know. I felt that she was treating me as all of the other girls did. Before her."

"All? You sound like you dated a chorus line."

He laughed. "No, it wasn't that many. Maybe six total. Seven. Do you count? Are you supposed to count?"

"How old are you?" I asked. He laughed. "Lucky, how did she and all the other five or six treat you?"

"Like a charity case."

I was chewing when he said it and continued chewing. His wheelchair was always on my mind, and this was only the second time we were together. I was just thinking about the damn thing. When I finished chewing, I took another bite, not ready to speak yet.

"Marilyn was the last one, and I just didn't feel like dating anymore after that. I hated being this novelty to women, treated as something fragile, someone incapable. I bought a ring for her and everything."

I put the rest of the sandwich in my mouth.

"I know where to get sex when I need it. Hey, your eyes just went wide. They sure are some pretty eyes. The mention of sex makes you uncomfortable?"

"How do you know that I am not seeing you as a charity case?"

He took a bite from his sandwich and chewed slowly, but he spoke before he finished chewing. "I don't think I care just yet."

"Why not?"

"Well, nothing's really happened yet, has it? If it gets serious, I'd start to care. Hope it gets serious."

"Do you think it will?"

"So far I like you."

"And if I see this as a good deed, we'd part ways. How do I know that I'm not a charity case to you?"

"Why would you think that? You're fit in every way."

"You're not the only one that's stared at around here."

"Ah. I don't care about that."

"I didn't say you did, but—I don't know—you could be feeling sorry for me, too."

"Naw, it's your eyes."

"Just my eyes? You do care enough that we're meeting out here in a field and not in town at a soda shop."

"You want a pickle?"

We talked until the food was gone. Until we tired of lounging on the blanket, we stayed there and bathed in the summer afternoon. We walked when we got tired of lying down and talked while walking, too. I pushed the wheelchair for a while and listened to Lucky go on and on about the best engines of all time, and later, we sat looking at nothing across the prairie. The sky stretched over us in a blue so clear it made my ears ring. "Here in the Great Plains," I told him, "you can see that the earth is round."

When our first official date had ended, we made plans to meet again. I asked him to find some chicken so that I could fry it up. I assured him that I'd be able to get away again. We were at the edge of the field to say our goodbyes. I knelt before him, trying my best to see him as my equal and to not feel pity for him. But it took some work because I was also trying to see myself as worthy of being equal to a white man. I checked my watch and saw that if I were to make the next bus, I'd have to leave soon. I told him as much. He pulled me toward him, his arms and hands stronger than I expected, and kissed me right on the lips. I resisted at first, but he just pressed harder, holding me closer in his hands. I kissed back to stop the fighting, but also because I wanted to. When he let go, I said, "I did not plan on kissing you, Janus Obeck. Don't force yourself on me."

"Hey, you remembered my real name."

"How could I forget a girl's name?"

"Oh, that again. Well?"

"Well what?"

"Did you enjoy it? Are you happy that it happened?"

"What did I say to you about courting, Lucky?"

"I forget. That it's old-fashioned?"

"You know what I said."

"Oh, but, Nella, I won't see you for a week."

"I hardly care."

"But I want you to care. Was it nice?"

"That's for me to know. I'll see you in a week." I pulled away and stood up, turned and walked quickly through the carrot-covered field. The plants were like Queen Anne's lace, but the smell more bitter. Like Queen Anne's, they were a little unforgiving to intruders, reaching their sticky and rough stems out to grasp at my nylons.

"Hey, don't leave that way. Are you coming back?"

I didn't turn around.

My heart kept beating wildly as I walked through the field. Of course, the speedy walk didn't help, but I felt for

Lucky in a way I hadn't felt for anyone else. His strength was surprising. Masculine. Amazing. I felt stereotypically safe in his arms. And since he was older (he still hadn't told me his age by that point, even though he promised to tell me the first time he kissed me), his face was rough from stubble. None of the boys my age back in Milwaukee were capable of any shadow, five o'clock or otherwise, so Lucky was fascinating. And the way he held me, the way he took complete control of that kiss, made me want to give him control. This all seemed cloying to me even then, but I couldn't help thinking about our meeting that way, about his kissing me, about me having kissed him back.

On the bus, I still wore the fedora. I had it low over my eyes and let it shield them as I nodded off a bit. I was woken when I felt something very real on my thigh. I let my eyes open slowly and saw some strange hairy white hand with scarred knuckles on my leg. It was such a large hand that it nearly covered my whole thigh. I wondered how a white man could sit next to a black girl on a public bus in Kansas without drawing any scrutiny. My heart was beating hard, and I felt an uncomfortable lump in my throat. I reclosed my eyes, hoping that I was dreaming, but I knew I wasn't. I considered starting up as if I were startled awake. Would that scare the man away? Should I scream and jump up? Should I pull the cord request-ing the bus to stop? I kept my eyes closed, too angry and frightened to look again. The man slid his hand farther up my leg, and it took all my nerves to not cry out, to not jump. Then he removed his hand from my leg altogether. I didn't open my eyes, but I heard him get up. The seat cushion sighed a little as his weight was lifted. But I stayed tense; my heart still raced.

"Tell you what, Frank," I heard him say. "These colored girls get prettier and prettier."

I listened to him walk away and down the bus aisle toward the front door.

"It used to be a time," some other voice said, Frank's undoubtedly, "when you could fuck 'em without consequence."

Involuntarily, I wiped at a bug on my face, pulled my hand away wet. It wasn't a bug. I prayed Frank and Hairy Hands didn't see me wipe.

"Oh, I don't know if that time is quite over yet," Hairy Hands said. He sounded sure as shit.

"Wonder where she's coming from," Frank mused. "Odd seeing coloreds out this way."

The bus slowed. The door opened.

"See you tomorrow, then?" Hairy Hands asked.

"If she's on again tomorrow, I'll let you drive."

Then Harry Hands got off the bus. The door closed and the bus started again.

Meeting Lucky this way wasn't going to work.

I needed a car. I sat there scheming about how to get one while my mother pressed my hair. She hummed as she worked, and I sat there bracing from potential grease burns if the Murray's pomade got too hot. The kitchen stank of burned hair, frying hair grease, and sweet potatoes candying. The heat from the stovetop competed with the heat of summer on the prairie.

"Are you okay with everything?" my mother asked. Her voice could be surprising to those who didn't know her, because it was soft and melodic, but she was a big woman. Not fat, just big. Tall, muscular, and intimidating. But her voice was the voice all mothers should have—like song, so easy to sooth or rile up, whatever the situation called for. Now, it was soothing.

"What do you mean? Living in Kansas?" And just like that, my way to a car just fell into my hair along with the pomade and the metal teeth of the pressing comb. "No, it's not okay."

"Are you lonely?"

"Of course. Not only are there no black people out here, but there are no kids. I mean, like me: teenagers. At least I can't find any. And it's so hard to get around here."

"You just haven't talked to those girls that I told you about yet. They exist. The buses pretty good around here, aren't they?"

"I guess they good if you like being on display. There was a little white girl who asked me if I had a tail the other day."

"You can ignore them."

The pressing comb sizzled as it burned through a patch of pomade. My mother drew the comb down a section of my hair, and I shrank away from the heat it created against my scalp. "You seventeen and you can't sit up straight while getting your hair hot-combed? Sit up, girl."

I sat up straighter and held my head as I thought she wanted me to. "I think I could use a car. I got my license before we left home. Even Daddy says I'm a pretty good driver."

"He do, but having a car is like having a baby. They a lot of responsibility. And I don't know if we have the money to afford another car."

"I can take care of it fine. I'll get a job somewhere."

"Uh-huh. Hold your ear down."

I held my ear, and my mother combed slowly through the edges right above my ear and temple, getting it straight as she could. Once the comb was through my hair, my mother said, "Nella, where did you get that fedora from?"

To buy me some time, I asked, "What, the hat?"

"Yes, the hat. Where did you get it? It looks kind of expensive."

"I found it. On the bus." I just told my mother a story.

"Really? Hope no white woman attacks you because you have her hat."

"I'm sure she won't, Ma."

"And where did you go to the other day?"

I was somewhat ready for that question and had concocted a complete story as an answer, but when I was presented with it, I wasn't prepared to lie aloud. Before Lucky, I was pretty honest with both of my parents and I told my mother everything, but that day I was going to tell her that I went window-shopping, walked around Liberty, bought some picnic food and made myself a little lunch right there in the park, but even though I'd just lied to her about the hat, I couldn't get the fabricated window-shopping story out. What I did say was "I don't know." It was a foolish thing to say—of course I knew where I was. My mother would see right through that one, I thought, so I quickly tried to rescind those words. "I walked a bit. Rode around on the bus. Got something to eat." It was not all a lie, really.

"Where? You can let go of your ear now. Sit up."

"Where?" She didn't believe me, and I said that silly statement again. "I don't know. All over Liberty, really. Rode with the bus to the edge of town."

"Don't be smart, Nella, it ain't becoming. Where did you get something to eat around here?"

"The grocery store."

"The grocery?"

"Just snacky type food."

"Huh. Hold your other ear down."

And I held it down. *Please don't ask anything else.* But she did.

"Where did you get the money from?"

"Huh?" I was so glad I couldn't see her face and she couldn't see mine. I knew she wasn't going to ask me again because it wasn't in her nature to ask questions twice. "I had some saved up."

"From where?"

She took the comb off the burner and waved it briefly. Smoke billowed out from its teeth. She dragged it across my hair. "Ow!" I yelled. She had burned the tip of my ear with the pressing comb. I had never been so happy to be in pain. She apologized repeatedly as I sucked in air through my teeth and ran to the sink to get some cold water to put on my ear. She was so distracted by the burn that she ended her inquisition.

After I took care of my burned ear, and after she finished my hair, my mother did not ask about my whereabouts, and I didn't offer to tell her. I suppose the whole conversation was forgotten, or she was saving it for another time. At dinner, my father asked me about my want of a car, so I supposed they talked about it with each other when I was in my bedroom. This seemed an unfair advantage to me, and I started to act sulky before any word of their decision. He, like Mama, said that cars were a lot of responsibility. "I can get a job to help take care of the car," I started. I wanted to start the argument off heavily in my favor so that it would be hard for them to knock down my defenses.

"Help take care of it?" my father asked. "If you get a car, Nella, you will completely take care of it. That car will be your pet."

"I'll take care of it, Daddy. What is there for me to do out here to get in trouble with the car?"

"Speaking of that, where can you work out here? It's all ma-and-pa operations. There's no getting in."

"It's got to be something I can do. Work at a shop somewhere or take in laundry—"

"Do what?" my mother asked.

"Laundry."

"Shut up. The only drawers you'll be washing is your own. This conversation is over."

I couldn't eat anymore. No one spoke. The only sounds were the flatware against the dishes and the wind blowing through the cracks of the wall.

"May I be excused?" I asked.

"When you finish your food," my mother answered.

I didn't move to eat, though. I sat there and sighed loudly. My father ignored me and started talking about work. Mama, taking cues from him, talked happily with him about his day. I sat there, looking stupid with my straight hair and my burned ear. My father talked about the buildings being constructed with WPA money. He was a structural engineer who was happy with his work in Milwaukee until he found out he was being paid a lot less than his coworkers, even those without the training or degrees. Daddy had lots of training during the war, especially in reconstruction in Europe, so he was a good fit for the WPA jobs. Now, he talked about the few black people he met while working and their wives and families. My mother was listening more for potential friends and dinner party attendees than my father's potential clients.

I couldn't care to listen because I was so angry. Over some white boy. I tried to tell myself that it wasn't over him, that it had more to do with freedom and friendship, but truthfully, it was because I wanted to be with Lucky. "I really hate it here," I said aloud.

"Nella, hush," my mother said.

"Really, really hate it here."

"It'll get better when school starts," my father said. "Isn't that in a few weeks?"

"You are acting like a child," my mother said. "Pouting like someone stole your turning top. Talking about doing white people's laundry."

"I didn't say white people."

"Your daddy didn't move us across the country so you can be washing no white folks' laundry."

"Just a few states over," Daddy said, "not across the country."

"Who said white folks?" I asked.

"Let's not be just as bad as them," Daddy said.

"You the one said there ain't no Negroes around here," my mother said. "Whose laundry was you going to do? You ain't doing nobody's laundry."

"Calm down, Raina."

"No, David, I've done that kind of daywork for years so she won't have to."

"Calm down."

"Maybe you can go back to Milwaukee for school," my mother said. Her voice was softer again. Kind, even. "Live with your grandmother. Would you like that?"

Would I like that? I wish I had a mirror in front of me because I had no idea what expression I gave my parents. I picked up my fork and looked down in my plate. I hoped to look like I was overjoyed about the possibility of Milwaukee, but still upset about the car. I scraped food around on my plate, played with the cooling syrupy sugar that covered the sweet potatoes. "Yeah," I said. "I'd like that," but of course, I did not. "But school is a long way off. And it'd be hard getting back this late."

"We can talk about it later. Since you're graduating, it's probably best for you to go back and finish off school there."

"Unless the schools are better here," my father said.

"Now, David, we talked about this." And there it was again: them deciding my life in my absence.

"You're really set on that car, ain't you?" Daddy asked. I nodded without looking up. "Maybe when you graduate from high school, but we just can't afford it right now."

"But I can pay for it if I get a job." I looked at him when I spoke. I felt so emotionally riled up I could have cried then.

"But we don't want you slaving for no white people," Mama said.

Then Daddy: "Besides, we want you to concentrate on your education. You have the opportunity to become something great. We have come a long way since your mama and I were kids. We have plans for you. Maybe you'll get into Spelman or Fisk. You could be a nurse or a schoolteacher. Why stop at that? Imagine it, Nella a doctor. There's no rush in growing up. You'll get a car eventually. And you can use the car when I'm home. For a short ride, that is."

I took another bite of candied yams. I moved the pulled pork around my plate, slowly chewed the yams. Their softness was unappetizing to me that day, though I usually loved them. "I'd really like to be excused."

"Go on, Nella."

I jumped up from my seat, taking my plate with me. I dumped the food in the trash, then went to my room. My head was slightly spinning, and I could still feel the sliminess of the sugar from the potatoes all over my tongue.

Milwaukee would be good: old friends and maybe some new ones, other people who look like me, parties to go to, dances to attend—in a word, a social life. But here, there was Lucky, whose blue eyes I hated to admit I admired, and his unassuming attitude and his kindness. There was him.

I had a little radio in my room. I turned it on and tried listening to some crooner, probably Sinatra, singing something about love, and then the voice of the horns, of the violins, and of the crooner eerily eased into the wind, whistling through the cracks of the old house.

There was some gangster on the radio when I woke up the next morning, my teeth feeling thick with last night's unfinished dinner. Although I went to bed early, I woke up late, or rather, I was woken up late. "It is almost eleven o'clock, honey," my mother said in her singsong voice. "Wake up, little one."

I sat up. I didn't know what it was like yet to wake up after drinking, but I imagined it was similar to the way I felt then. My head hurt, my skin was raw and covered with fabric fold impressions from sleeping in my street clothes, and I was already annoyed with the day. "It's summer, ain't it?"

"Yeah, but you have things to do. You know, ride the bus? Eat picnic lunches you bought with money you somehow saved?"

I said nothing.

"Well, don't go too far. Your dad wants to talk to you when he returns."

When she left my room, I undressed for a bath. I hadn't planned on seeing Lucky that day, but I was to call him at lunchtime. I bunched my hair atop my head and wrapped a towel around it to keep the humidity out, then went to run the bathwater.

While I waited for the tub to fill, my mother came to tell me to have lunch on my own. She said that she had plans with the women's group at the church. There were two other Negro women whose families had homesteaded in Seward County years ago. They became fast friends with my mother because of their color and their religion more than anything else. Each woman had children my age, but they were always busy about the farm and too reluctant to talk to a city girl like me. I wanted to get to know Vivian, one of the women's daughters who was a year older than me, but she was always busy taking care of her younger siblings and doing other domestic jobs around their farm. Maybe, I told myself, if I had a relationship with some of the local children, I'd feel more welcome in Kansas all around. Maybe Milwaukee wasn't what I wanted.

My mother gave me a couple of dollars. "There's food here, but in case you want something else, you won't have to go into your savings."

I sucked my teeth at her.

It was such a hot day that I was sweating before I got in the tub. I couldn't get used to the Kansas heat and the lack of a lake breeze. But I had to admit that I preferred the heat to the cold. I didn't want to deal with another Wisconsin winter. Ever. It was summer here, but it got cool in the evenings, and I couldn't know what winter would be like in Kansas. And if I were to stay here, what would school be like for me? I would stick out, that's for sure, being one of a very few black kids. Or maybe there were other colored homesteaders and family farmers around with farm-loads of kids. And weren't schools segregated in Kansas?

I dressed quickly. I rolled my hair up into two big French rolls, which looked overly fancy for my everyday clothes. I didn't care. Who did I have to impress? When I finished getting ready, I grabbed some bread from the kitchen and made my way to the nearest phone, eating as I walked.

I went to the drugstore in town and went to the back entrance. I asked about the phone softly, politely.

"You here just 'bout every day, ain't you, girl?"

I kind of smiled, but not really. I still didn't know what the proprietor looked like because I never looked right at him.

"Give me a nickel," he said. "Naw, wait. Is this important, girl?"

"Yes, sir."

"Then give me a dime. Important calls are a dime."

I cursed him to myself. Then I cursed myself—I had forgotten to bring change. I only had the two dollar bills my mother gave me.

"Ain't got a dime?"

I nodded slowly. "I have my mother's money," I said. "Supposed to get some bread and some meat, sir, and I need to take the bus to meet her."

"She can't see you a dime?"

"I suppose so. Just have to get less meat." Lying was becoming easier. I was losing my morals for some white boy.

"Well, I don't want to take food from nobody. Not even folks like you. What your mother give you?"

I wondered if the bills were folded together or not, if I could free a single without revealing both bills. "A dollar, sir."

"A dollar! That'd buy a lot of bread and meat."

I dared to look up at him. Slowly. Opened my eyes as wide as his type imagined them to be. Tried to look like a hurt animal.

"Give it here. I'll give you back your change."

I slid the dollar out of my pocket easily, pushing back the other bill as if I were peeling a banana. I gave him the crisp single, continued to act like an animal: shy and bunnyish. Dependent. He snatched it from me and took it to his till. "Can you count?" he asked.

"Yes, sir."

"Colored folks know too much nowadays as far as I'm concerned." He came back with the change and counted, out loud, ninety-five cents into my palm. But he'd given me only three quarters, a dime, and a nickel. What now? I could not get used to that brand of racism and knew then and there that I'd be returning to Milwaukee in the fall, Lucky be damned. I said nothing. Just continued to hold my hand out.

"You know where the phone is," he said.

"I'm afraid," I said carefully, "that I'm missing a nickel."

"Did you pocket that nickel and try to snow me?" he asked, shouting. I heard someone behind him laughing, a customer, undoubtedly, having a soda at the counter.

"No, sir," I said. I did not move my hand. And I looked right at him. No doe eyes this time. He looked back.

After a short minute, he said, "Oh. Seems I have forgotten to give it to you." He dropped the nickel into my hand. "Next time you come around here, you bring a dime, you hear me?"

"Thank you," I said, dropping the *sir*. I then walked briskly to the telephone and dialed for Lucky. He answered on the second ring.

"It's good to hear your voice," he said. "Want to make a date for tomorrow?"

"I think so. We have to talk about something."

"We haven't been together long enough to have to talk."

"Yeah, well, things happen fast in my life. I need to find another way out there, too."

"No bus anymore?"

"The bus was a little uncomfortable."

"Surely you can deal with a little discomfort to see me."

"I don't want to have to explain it."

He was silent before asking if I was still interested in him. I told him yes, that the talk had no bearing on our relationship, really. He was skeptical, but he moved on to another point. "I was thinking that, maybe, we can do something different. I'm not sure yet how this would work, but I love taking dates out to the movies."

"Yeah, I'm not sure how that would work, either."

"We can figure something out. Will you take a bus tomorrow?"

"Yes, I have to."

"Maybe I can meet you there in town."

"Are you crazy?"

"No, I'm not. Listen, I have a great idea."

"Hush. I think I've gotten my father around to get me a car."

"A car? Is that right?"

"You still on that phone, girl?" the drugstore operator called from his station behind the counter.

"Let's just meet at our regular place tomorrow," I said into the receiver.

"How would you all afford another car?"

"We'll just talk about it tomorrow. See you then. Should we meet around eleven?"

"Eleven will be fine."

"If I'm not there by quarter after, don't expect me."

"Of course, as usual."

"Some other folks may want to use the phone," the druggist said.

I sighed heavily, heard my breath amplified in the mouthpiece as it bounced back to me. There was only one other customer in the drugstore, the one who was always there sucking down phosphate after phosphate.

"See you tomorrow," I said quickly. Lucky said good-bye, and I hung up the phone and left the drugstore.

Outside, it was bright and sunny. Plants were still green, and some of the people who passed me on the street smiled at me sincerely, in spite of their being white. The drugstore felt dingy and musky. Every time I went there to call Lucky, I'd go back outside expecting rain, because there was nothing but gloom in that place. Each time the sun was shining, and each time I was often taken aback by its blatant glare.

The rest of the afternoon, I spent window-shopping. I bought popcorn from a stand and a Pepsi from a machine and walked around, entertaining myself. I considered going to a movie, but there wasn't a picture on that I wanted to see. Just looking at the marquee, I thought of what Lucky said about going on a movie date, and I laughed a little too loudly. The ticket holder heard me and asked if I needed any help. I told him no, that I was thinking about seeing the replay of *A Night in Casablanca*. Then I walked on down the street.

I heard someone beep behind me, two friendly toots, and turned to find my mother riding in an old Packard with two other women. They beckoned me over.

"You are a mighty fine-looking child," one of the women said.

"You'd work good on the farm," said the other, "but you look too citified with those two rolls in your hair."

"You mean she looks too grown," my mother said. "We beeped to offer you a ride, Nella. You up for it?"

"I guess so."

"Well, then hop in," said the woman behind the wheel. "It's hot outside."

I slid into the back next to Mama. The two others reintroduced themselves to me, just in case I had forgotten who they were, which I hadn't. One was Mrs. Jackie Taylor. She was the one with Vivian as a daughter. I briefly asked after Vivian and learned that she was just fine and that I should go see her sometime. Mrs. Georgia Cox had two daughters around my age, but I'd yet to meet them. While we rode along and the jazz singers talked about the old days on the radio, my mother held me close and stroked my hair. She hummed so softly, the ladies up front probably couldn't hear her, but I heard her, and it was soothing.

At home, my mother washed dishes, and I dried. She now believed that I was only wandering around the other day, riding the bus and window-shopping, because she had witnessed me doing just that. Now, she talked to me about returning to Milwaukee for school. I said that the idea sounded good, but I wasn't sure. "I want to try this place out, you know? Plus, I don't want to be so far away from you and Daddy."

"Milwaukee ain't that far."

"Hey, I was in the car on the way here. It's far." We also talked about living with my grandmother. My father's mother was down in Louisiana. I'd be staying with Grandma Thompson, who was an overly neat woman who wanted everyone and everything around her as tidy as could be. "I love her dearly," I said. "You know that."

"I know, so there won't be a problem."

"Grandma can spot a crumb in the next room, even if you don't see it. And she'll natter you on it until you pick it up," I said.

"She's just a little old."

"I know, but I'm afraid I would clash with her too much."

My father had come in. I didn't look up when he did, but just kept looking down at the dishes, wiping each one dry. I spoke to him but didn't raise my head. My mother said something else about her mother, something about how she had turned out all right being raised by Grandma Thompson. I sincerely cannot remember what she said. I just remember that the dishes stopped coming my way and that I looked up to see my mother beaming at me like she had suddenly discovered the meaning of life. I looked past her at my father, standing there with a brand-new bike. He looked proud enough to have sired it.

Again, I wished I had a mirror in front of me so that I could see my expression. A bike. I knew I should have looked happy—they both had decided that a bike was the next best thing to a car. They saw it as some kind of transportation, a vehicle that was easy to maintain and practical. My mother went to stand next to my father, who still held the bike proudly before him. My mother ran a hand along the frame as if she were with it in a showroom, seducing me with its chrome.

How was I to ride that thing all the way to meet Lucky? And once I got there, in this heat, I'd be wet in sweat. My hair would sweat out, too, and frizz up. It would kink up all over again.

"It's got front shock absorbers, so it should be a smooth ride on these country roads," Daddy said, as if he were trying to sell it to me. He lifted the front end up by the handlebars and let it fall and bounce back from the floor, his hands never too far from the handlebars just in case. "And look at this." He pointed his head to the back of the bike. "Vented rear fender."

I looked at the vent. It seemed useless on the bike. The bike seemed useless.

"Honey, it's not a car," my mother said, "but it'll do, right?"

They were waiting for my approval. I forced a smile on my face and tried to appear happy. That fake smile sincerely smoothed things out, though; it would do. I'd have to make it do. It was better than the bus, for sure. It was better than nothing. I'd just take it slow when I went to meet Lucky. I placed the drying towel on the kitchen counter and went to my father. I kissed him on his mouth and on both his cheeks. When I finished thanking him, I backed away from Dad and took a good look at the bike.

It was a Hawthorne, with matching red-and-white tassels on the handlebars. I grabbed the handlebars first and bounced the bike up and down a bit, as my father did, to get a feel for the features. It was a way around town that wasn't hitchhiking or the bus.

"I love you both," I said. Mama obviously knew that the bike was coming. "It ain't a car, but it'll do. Thank you very much."

"Don't say 'ain't,' dear," Mama said.

It was now fully summer. Lucky and I had a routine: I would ride right out to the outskirts of town and he'd pick me up. I took each bike ride slow, stopping and walking the bike if I felt myself sweating too much, so I wouldn't be a mess when we met. We also went on the occasional movie date. Lucky had bought me a nurse's uniform, which I wore whenever we wanted to go to a show. I'd act as his nurse and we'd sit near the aisle, him in his wheelchair. No one suspected anything, as far as we knew.

Lucky had done something else, something much more romantic than movie dates. He bought us a tree. "It's a basswood tree. It'll grow big and it'll grow fast. Lots of shade from basswoods."

"What would we do with that?" I asked.

"We'll plant it in my field. I mean, our field. And it'll be our tree. Isn't that neat?"

"If you say so." It was in the bed of his truck, the roots in a burlap sack. My bike rested beside it. It looked like a happy little tree. "Lucky, we need to talk."

"You know, you said that once before, but we never got around to talking."

I sat on the bumper of his truck. "It's the same subject. Nothing's changed."

"So it's not about the tree. It couldn't be because you just found out about it."

"In a way, it's about that tree. Remember when I told you that I asked my parents for a car?"

"Yep. The next day you came over riding the bike, and I told you that was an odd-looking car."

"Yes, the bike is part of it, too." I looked out at the wildflowers in the field, clover and milkweed, wild carrots and black-eyed Susans. The grass was tall and blew in the prairie breeze. I took a deep breath in and steeled myself against what I was going to say. As I talked, I focused on where the grasses met the horizon. "My argument to them was that I needed a car to get around to do things and that I was bored. I said I'd work for it."

"And they got you a bike." His voice was soft and flat. He knew that he wouldn't like what was coming. "Yeah, but they also offered to send me back to Milwaukee for the school year." I didn't look at him when I said it, so I don't know how he took it at first. I did know that he was uncharacteristically silent. "I didn't say no, that I didn't want to go." He was still quiet. "I didn't say yes, either. I don't know what I want."

When he still had not spoken, I looked at him, and his face was blank. I felt angry in a flash. "Hey, look, Lucky, there's nothing here for me. I don't have any friends or anything. It's boring as dirt. There are actual tumbleweeds!"

Lucky moved around me and got out of his chair and onto the bed of his truck, using the tailgate for support and hoisting himself up on it. He wouldn't say anything. He walked to the tree sapling and grabbed it by its base right above the burlap bag. "You think you can help me with this?"

I clucked my teeth and then jumped up on the back of the truck. "I'm almost done with high school, you know, and I want my time there to be special. I want to go to dances. I want to be doing something with other people. I'll repeat it—there's nothing for me here."

I had grabbed the tree as I talked, and together, we let it down off the back of the truck. Lucky made his way to the ground first, climbing from it to his chair. I jumped down after him, still complaining and arguing. Finally, he said, "Nothing for you here? No friends?"

And my anger was gone. "You know what I mean."

"Let's plant this tree."

Because I might be leaving for the school year, Lucky and I spent hours together in August, lying next to our little basswood sapling, holding each other, getting further each day in our heavy petting routine. The times were idyllic. When we were at the garage, and the days were slow and summery, we dared to get closer. I revealed more skin, and Lucky didn't talk so much. Only our breathing was loud. It was as exciting as imaginable, but still innocent.

Those idle days for us were ideal for mischief by others. It was the quiet in thrillers, when the hero's guard is down and he's happy in love. That's when the killer strikes. Or the attackers. But I think only one raped me.

Lucky and I had just got done with one of our make-out sessions in his garage. I had stopped it before we went too far, and we were both still sweating and feeling dreamy. We dressed, and I went to his desk to look at some magazines I'd brought along. He got on his creeper and scooted beneath some old jalopy. We were behaving like an old married couple.

Usually, when a car drove up, I'd have to get up and grab the broom to make like I was sweeping, or put on my nursing hat. That day was no exception. I was moving languidly, though, like a fat-full kitten, and probably didn't look like I was doing work. They were in a late-model car, probably a Ford. I can't remember, and Lucky didn't get a look at it because he was beneath that old car. There were three of them, all dressed in golf shirts and baggy pants with gold chains. The lead one, the one who raped me for sure, was blond as they came and full of brown freckles. His eyes were pale blue and his skin soft and pliable. The one to his right, who may have had something to do with me, too, was dark haired with flawless skin. He looked like Hollywood bad guys do. Just looking at him and his dark eyes made me grab the broom tighter. The other one was obviously the lesser one, less in intelligence at least. His hair was dark, but not as dark as Bad Guy to the right. He was a short man and broad chested like an ape, his arms bowed out as if he was used to heavy lifting.

"You the only one here, girl?" Blond said. His voice was soft but menacing. When I heard it, I wanted to go away directly. It was clear that these guys were up to no good. I didn't answer him, but Lucky slid from beneath the car he was working on and sat up best he could.

"What can I do for you? She's my help and my nurse."

"Well, hello, nurse," said the little one. I sucked my teeth in spite of myself. The tsking sound I made was loud in the silence of the garage.

"Gentlemen," Lucky said. "Can I help you?" I saw that Lucky sensed trouble, too. The dark-haired one cracked his neck by quickly leaning his head to the side and back up again.

"What do you need a nurse for?" Blond asked.

I leaned the broom against the wall and said, meekly as I could, "Would you like for me to get your chair, sir?"

"Sure thing, Nurse Nella."

"Nella," the little one said. "Nurse Nella." His voice annoying and useless; he seemed to be talking just to be talking.

"I don't get around too good," Lucky said to the men.

The three of them came all the way into the garage, moving in sync with one another and keeping their positions. I kept an eye on them as I went for Lucky's chair. I rolled it over to him and then helped him up and into it. I backed away from him, back toward the broom and away from the three men.

"She's not dressed like a nurse," Blond said.

"Is there something wrong with your car?" Lucky asked. He smiled, sizing them up. This was too easy for them. I wanted to sit down there and give up, but I didn't know what we'd be giving up yet.

"Out of gas," Blond said, nodding back with his head but not taking his eyes away from me. "Didn't know colored nurses could care for good white boys. Now did you know that, fellers?"

"No," the other two answered in unison. They all looked at me as if I were an Easter ham on display, but Blond's eyes lingered more. I recognized the hate there—I'd seen enough of that in my seventeen years directed right at me—but there was also lust. I remembered the man on the bus, the one only I and the bus driver knew about. My knees got watery.

"I thought they were all supposed to look like fat mammies," Blond said. The other two laughed good-naturedly, and the Blond asked, "Do you ever get to lay her? Hm?"

I backed away. Lucky didn't answer. The mean one with black hair came swiftly around his boss, around Lucky, to me, and stood beside me. Daring me to move.

"I asked if you fuck her, you gimp."

"Answer him," the short one said. I jerked reflexively.

"I'm going to ask you gentlemen to leave. She may be colored, but she's still my nurse. And she's still a woman."

The little one darted at Lucky and punched him in the stomach, so quick neither one of us could have seen it coming. It winded Lucky for a minute; he doubled over in his chair and groaned loudly. I cried his name and stepped toward him, but Bad Guy grabbed me and held me tight by the wrists with just one of his large hands. He slapped me with the other, his full hand connecting hard to my face. The sound echoed throughout the garage. I screamed in pain, for help.

"Mind if I . . . ?" Blond asked. He didn't wait for an answer. Lucky sat up and swung out and hit Lesser Man in the jaw. Lesser Man was fazed, but not for long. Some-how, Lucky struggled with him and tried to fling him away. Bad Guy passed me off to Blond, who took me and then quickly threw me on the floor. I scrambled away, screaming still, and tried to get over to Lucky so that he could help me (although, really, what could Lucky have done?), but Blond grabbed one of my ankles and dragged me toward him. I felt the skin on my knees and one of my elbows being scratched by the concrete floor. Before I turned away from Lucky, I saw Bad Guy punch him across the temple. I screamed again. Blond put his hand over my mouth, and I bit at him, but he turned his hand so that the edge was in my mouth, pushed it so that I gagged.

I could hear Lucky grunt each time he was hit. Couldn't see him. I could also hear those two bastards as they hollered insults at him. Too, I heard skin connecting with skin, wet and slick, slapping noises, thuds like meat on the butcher's block. I was sure that they were trying to kill him.

Blond had my shirt ripped open. My skirt was pushed up and around my waist. "Open your eyes," he said. "I want you to see that I'm the one fucking you."

I closed my eyes tighter. He took his hand from my mouth and whipped me across the face. With my mouth free again, I screamed. Lucky couldn't help me, and no one was around to hear me, but I screamed. He kneed me in my stomach. I heard him undo his pants.

"Open your fucking eyes," he said.

I opened my eyes. I saw him holding his penis. I saw it purpled against his pale skin. I saw the elastic band of his underwear. I saw his belt undone and the buckle hanging off to the side, rocking with him. I heard the metal of the buckle parts clink against each other. I heard the two men Lucky wrestled with laughing over his sobs, and the disconcerting sounds of a man's sobs were too jarring. Lucky's crying made me feel more helpless, made me realize the trouble I was in.

"You see this?" Blond asked. He held his penis in his hand toward me. "Will this be your first time? I hope so. I hope every time you fuck again, you'll think of me."

I squirmed, tried to move my knees, tried to move him off me. I closed my eyes again, and he punched me in the middle of my face. The connection forced my head against the concrete floor of the garage. I involuntarily opened my eyes. The sting was so great that I could not see. Stars—really, little beams of light—spiraled out from the center, shooting like arrows. The garage and its contents, the people in it, came back. I looked at Blond and saw him doubled, wavy. And when he forced himself in me, I felt the sudden burn and dull ache of skin breaking. Overwhelmed with the pain and stress, I got sick and spewed all over him. He slapped me again.

And in this way, I lost my virginity. Admittedly and ashamedly, I tried to reach back to that euphoric post-copulating feeling I had from being with Lucky earlier. I tried to go blank and imagine it was Lucky, tried to ignore the ripping of the skin in and around my vagina. My body—probably to protect itself—responded to the moves of sex. I got wet. Oh, I despised every minute of it mentally, and my body crawled with hate, but there it was: sex. Unwanted and ugly, and happening anyway.

And when he was in me, the violence didn't end. Each time I closed my eyes, I was punched in the gut. So I had to see this freckled-face man, filled with as much contempt for me as I was for him, rocking above me. I didn't even know if I was screaming anymore, but my throat was scratchy and hot, my face streaming with tears, and sweat—our sweat—and the spit that flew from his mouth, and puke, and blood.

At some time, I blacked out. I think I opened my eyes to see dark hair, and when I opened them again, Lucky was there beside me, his face puffy and purple, bleeding and pitiful. I hurt all over, and I'm sure he did, too. I cried right away, and Lucky's face folded from my tears. "I'm so sorry," he said. And this made me cry louder.

I made myself calm down long enough to say, "You don't hate me?"

He slid a little closer to me and brought his hand to my face, kissed me. "I can never hate you," he said. "Why would I hate you?"

"Because if I wasn't here, this wouldn't have happened to you."

"I don't know about that. Those guys were looking for some kind of trouble. Nella, this is not your fault. Look, we need to call someone. We need help."

"Who? What would we tell them?"

"The truth?"

"Oh, Lucky, the truth is a little socially unacceptable."

"I don't know then."

"I can't think. What if the cops around here know them?"

"It's okay. Yeah, we're kind of in a situation, aren't we?"

I thought of how the towns nearby were small. Very few people lived here. "Did you recognize any of them?"

Lucky shook his head. "No. I tried to place them, but they aren't from Kismet."

My crying had subsided to a whisper. Lucky's breathing was calm. I thought he was sleeping when he asked, "How are you feeling?"

I tried lifting my head, and it felt as if it had been pounded against the concrete floor. I'm sure it felt that way because it had been pounded against the floor. My vagina burned, my inner thighs ached and were rubbed raw, and my stomach hurt from Blond's constant punching. "Hurt all over," I said. "Even the edges of my lips are sore from his pressing his hand into my mouth. I feel like he . . ." and I was going to say *he bit me*, but I didn't want to upset Lucky more. I tried to remember if Blond did bite me, and I got a flash of his eyes and the hate there. I closed my eyes against it, then opened them again on Lucky. "You? How are you feeling?"

"This is kind of serious," he said. He sat up a little on his elbows, looked at me in the eyes, and said, "I don't think I'll be walking again."

"Oh, Lucky." I punched out at him and laughed. The laughter hurt me physically, but it also felt like relief. "We shouldn't be joking."

He smiled back at me. "But I love your smile."

"It's probably pretty battered right now."

"It's more beautiful than ever, Nella. Can you get up, you think?"

Instead of answering, I sat up slowly. My shirt was done, ripped into strips of fabric that ineffectively covered odd areas of skin. My bra was split in two. My skirt was soiled with blood and goo. A mess. I felt like crying again. "They did a number on us, didn't they, Luck?"

"Ain't no luck about it. Suppose there's bad luck. Are you okay yet?"

I nodded. Then I rolled over so that I was on all fours. From there, I stood slowly. Each pang of pain I had, I sucked air in through my teeth. "I don't know how we'll explain this."

"Me neither. I'm going to need you to call my sister. She's a nurse of sorts."

"Is she?"

"That is, she is not a nurse, but she knows a lot about pain and healing."

"What would she say? About?" I pointed at him, then me, then did it again.

"She has had her share of weird relationships. Not weird, but you know."

I gasped. "She was with a black man?"

"No. Nothing like that. I'll tell you another day."

"Okay, I'll call your sister. But what will I tell her? Do I tell her everything over the phone?"

"No, no. Just tell her that I've been hurt and that she should come by. Tell her that you need clothes."

"And what do I say when she asks who I am?"

"She probably won't, but if she does, just say you're a friend. That's not a lie, right? We're still friends, right?"

"Of course. When she gets here, what do we tell her?"

"Everything, I guess. We'll have to come clean to her, at least. It's not a big deal, really. I mean what happened is, but telling Greta is not. I think she already suspects something—she's been making these huge lunches for me, and I keep finishing it all. Except for some days, and those are the days when you're gone."

"Okay. I'll give her a call."

Lucky was right. Greta, his sister, didn't ask who I was. She was there as quick as her pickup could carry her. She had Lucky in his wheelchair in no time, and we were both cleaned and bandaged up within an hour. Without prompting, Lucky told her that we'd been seeing each other for some time. She didn't blink an eye. She did say, once the incident was relayed to her and we were all cleaned up, "We'll have to tell your parents."

"You see," I said, "I was thinking of telling them that I was in a terrible accident with my bike. I was thinking of finding some hidden bluff or something."

Greta shook her head. "You might be pregnant."

"She's right," Lucky said. "I hadn't thought of that."

"Besides that, you both look like crap," Greta said. "You're probably a looker on your good days, but today ain't one of your good days." Greta grabbed my chin and turned my face left and right. "You don't look too bad. I guess the bluff thing may work, but do you want to hurt your bike? You'd have to hurt your bike."

"I don't want to hurt the relationship I have with Lucky, either."

"Good luck with that one, huh?"

"I know it sounds ridiculous, but it may be our best bet. You don't know my parents. If they find out something like this happened to me, they would keep me under watch until I'm married. Or they will ship me off to Milwaukee so fast that we'd all forget I was even here. If they find out about Lucky," I started, but I stopped. Would Daddy hurt Lucky? Would they call the cops on us, and if so, why? Why was what Lucky and I doing illegal? "I don't know what to do," I said.

"I can't think of a better solution than to tell your folks."

I couldn't get over this woman. She was much bigger than Lucky, and I was sure it had nothing to do with his disability. It was just that she was a huge woman and very maternal. She looked more like his mother than his sister. But because she was so accepting of me and Lucky, and because she had had an intriguing clandestine relationship or two that I'd yet to learn about, I liked her. "So what do I do? Bike home and tell them what happened?"

"I can take you home," she said. I was already shaking my head.

"No," I said. "We can't tell them. I don't know what I will say, but it sure won't be that I was beaten and raped by three white men while I was visiting my white boyfriend."

"So you want to tell them you got hurt on your bike?" she said.

"I don't know." I held my head in exasperation. "No offense, Lucky, but I'm tired of lying for you."

"What do you mean?" Lucky asked.

"Never mind. I have to tell them the truth, right? Or some version of it. It doesn't matter."

"What doesn't matter?" Greta asked.

I waved my hand. I didn't know what I was talking about.

"You feeling okay?" she asked.

"I am very tired. My head hurts."

"Would you like some water?"

I nodded.

"We'll get you water, then we'll get you home."

Greta's pickup truck bounced on every pebble on the road. Each bounce shook me, and each shaking hurt. "Slow down, sis," Lucky said.

I sat between them, and I couldn't help but touch and be touched by both Lucky and Greta during the trip. I kept crying from the physical pain and the fear I had of my parents. Every time I cried, Lucky and Greta would pat my thigh.

"They are not going to hate you," Greta said. "They will be upset, probably more with Lucky than with anyone else, and of course the rapist—"

"Greta, put a little something sweet on that, okay? Let's not talk about those guys so graphically right now. Nella's still here."

"I didn't say anything graphic, Lucky, I just called him by what he is. He raped her so he is a rapist."

"Okay, sis, get to your point."

"The point is that they won't hate you. You didn't do anything wrong, really. Why didn't you two call the cops again?"

"Because she's black, Greta."

"Well," she said, then added, "I suppose so," and I wasn't sure what she was talking about. "Guess it was best to call me or someone like me. It worked all right, yeah?"

I started crying again.

"She still has to tell her parents," Lucky said. I nodded my head up and down. Even that motion hurt.

We were quiet for the rest of the trip, except for me navigating the way to my house here and there. When we pulled onto my street, I started crying. I let a thick sob escape, and again I was throttled by the tears. When we were about two blocks from my house, I said, "I can't do this. Please pull over here."

"We have to," Greta said, but she pulled over as I asked. Lucky didn't say a word. He didn't touch me or comfort me in any way. I looked at him, almost angry with him. I could see that the muscles in his face were tense, that his jaw was clenched. I could see swelling all over from the fight and bruises the color of old fruit.

"Maybe I should go in alone."

"If you go alone," Lucky said, "I would never see you again."

"Why do you think we'll see each other if we all go together? Oh, hi, Mama and Daddy, this is my boyfriend, Lucky, and his sister, Greta. Lucky and I were just beaten by three strange men, but now, they're just dropping me off."

"Raped, too," Greta said.

"Greta!" Lucky said to her, yelling. She sighed. She shut off her truck. We three sat in the cab not talking, but I could hear how loud our thoughts were. After some time, Greta asked, "How far is your house from here?"

I pointed up the road. "About a block and a half."

"Should I drive up? I could talk to your parents."

"Do I look bad?"

"What do you mean?" Lucky asked.

"I mean that I'm not that beat up in the face, am I? I can say I fell. I can say that it got too dark and I fell. Lucky, I probably won't be able to see you for a while."

"But I want to see you, Nella, especially after what happened to us."

"That's why I won't be able to see you. I can't raise any suspicion from my parents."

"You're not going to tell them," Greta said.

"I can't do that," I answered.

"But what if you're pregnant?"

"We'll deal with that when we get there. Or I will."

"Have you and Lucky ever had sex?"

Who the fuck is this lady? "No!"

"That means you won't have any qualms about aborting the baby, if we can find someone."

"Oh my good Lord," I said.

"Greta," Lucky said, "some tact, please."

"If she's pregnant, I mean. I only meant if, honey."

I didn't respond to her. She raised her hand to my face slowly. I felt like a horse being viewed, the way she peered at me. Her hand softly touched my bruises. She grabbed my chin, then gently turned my face toward her.

"You don't look too bad in this light," she said. "A little beat up, but there is tenderness you feel, right?" I nodded. "We may not see it." She spoke while still holding my chin. She then let go and pressed lightly against the bruises. "I suppose this could look like a bike fall. Don't say a bluff, though, because we'd have to hurt your bike."

"Then I won't say a bluff."

"If you say you were tripped up on something in the night, you won't be able to go out at night for a while."

"I understand. And I don't plan on seeing Lucky."

Lucky touched my shoulder and I turned to him. "Are we—is this over? You and I?"

"No. We're just on hold."

"But this is when I need you. Nella, look what the fuck we just been through back there."

"Maybe it's best, then, that we take a break."

"I won't ever see you again, will I?"

"I didn't say that." I couldn't read his face through all the blue and purple that covered it. I heard the driver's-side door open and knew it was time for me to get out. I reached out and placed a hand on Lucky's cheek. "Don't mess up my words."

"I love you, Nella."

"I think that's the adrenaline talking," I said. I kissed him quickly, but softly, careful not to hurt his lips. I slipped out from Greta's side, and once on the sidewalk, I turned and waved at Lucky and his sister. Greta started the engine and I walked away.

My parents said hello nonchalantly when I walked in and tried to continue to my bedroom, but my mother called me back. "It's almost ten, Nella, where you been?"

"Just out and riding around."

"Come here. What you hiding? Look at me." She stood up and faced me. She winced a little and reached out. "What happened here? Your cheek. Your lip. Nella, what happened to you?"

My father stood up and came to look at my face. "What is it?" he said.

I told my lie, feeling tired of lying to my mother but, worse, feeling like I didn't want her to touch me. His hands were too large, too present in memory, and too heavy. When my mother reached out and touched my shoulder, I couldn't help but think of Blond. My mind's eye saw short hair. My crotch felt the pain from violently losing my virginity. The day resurged and I reacted. I pushed away from my mother. Recoiled. "There was a stone in the road," I said. "Couldn't see because it was getting dark."

"A stone," she echoed.

I nodded.

"You were on your bike?"

I nodded.

"Did you fall on your face?" Daddy said.

"Does it look that bad?" I said. "Not directly on my face, no. My shoulder."

"Oh," my mother said. She let go of me.

"How's the bike?" Daddy said.

"David, really. She's hurt."

"The bike's fine. I ain't that hurt."

My mother drew in closer to me and looked at my face. "You've been acting odd lately," she said. "Foggy. Where you get that shirt from?"

"Oh, this?" I held up the shirttail of Greta's outsized blouse. "I've had it." My stomach audibly bubbled.

"You're hungry," my mother said. She placed her hand on one of my shoulders and whatever I had eaten earlier threatened to reappear. I swallowed.

"I'm fine."

"You probably weren't paying attention," my father said.

"It was getting dark," I said. "I think I would like to lie down."

My mother reached out and touched my face. I winced and backed away. "Maybe you've had a concussion," she said. "Should we take her to the hospital?"

A quick flash of a learned doctor popped into my mind, of some man telling my parents that my story didn't follow, that the bruises were all wrong. "I'll be fine. I just need to rest."

"What's the bike like? Is that all broken up, too?"

"Oh, David, I don't believe you! Our daughter just had a fall on her face and you still going on about the bike."

"The bike is fine. I fell; it did not."

"Baby, I'm sorry," my father said. "I wasn't thinking."

"You sure the hell was not. Go lie down, Nella, if you need to. I'll be up soon with a glass of water. Would you like that, honey? A glass of water?"

"Yes, ma'am." I walked around my mother, nodded at my father, and then went to the stairs. I walked up to my room and went inside. Trying not to think of the day and trying not to cry, I got dressed. Doing so, I could see glimpses of my face in the mirror. The bruises weren't as bad as I thought, but they were there. There was a small cut beneath my eye. That eye itself was black, burgundy, and a little puffy. Another cut was across the bridge of my nose, mostly on the left side. There was another scrap on my cheek. That was from the floor of the garage, from when Blond had pushed my face against the concrete. I felt my face scrape against the ground, as a child's knee would when she fell off a bike.

Later, with my shirt off, I saw blackened splotches on my breasts and stomach. Teeth marks. When I took off my panties blood was in the seat, and it was nowhere near time for my period. But still, I held back crying because my mother would be up to say good night. I continued to get ready for bed, picking long pajamas so that my arms and legs would be covered and hide any other scrapes.

About a minute after I got in bed, my mother knocked on the door. I invited her in, and she came with a glass of water and a big cookie on a plate. She set these on the bedside table and sat down on the bed next to me. She said nothing at first, but only looked over my face. I watched her eyes trace the bruises and scratches.

I sat up in bed and took the water. I drank some. My face hurt. It felt as if everything had to come forward on my face in order to drink, and it all ached. The water was cool and flat against the pain and pierced little slivers of ice in my head.

"Fell off your bike."

I nodded. She was too close to me, too hot. I repositioned myself so she wouldn't be touching my leg with her hip, but instead of staying where she was, she scooted in closer and put a hand on my knee.

"Some long pajamas for this time of year. You cold?"

I shrugged.

"Nella, I want you to know you can be honest with me."

"I am honest."

"You can tell me anything, Nella."

"You think I'm not telling you something?"

"I know sometimes I seem mean and sometimes I get upset, but I can help you."

"Mama, I know. I fell. Like I said."

"Would you like to go to Milwaukee right away? Maybe Kansas ain't right for you at all."

Would I like to go? I wasn't sure how to answer that question. "I don't know."

"We both want you to be happy, and we want what's best for you."

"I know."

"You can always tell me the truth."

"You said that."

"Don't be smart, Nella. I love you and care for you, but it's best to tell me what really happened before I find out myself."

"I fell off my bike."

She stood up. "Okay. You have sweet dreams, baby girl."

"I will."

She left, leaving me to think about the dreams I knew I'd have. I took another sip of water, freely wincing at the pain. I put the glass down and picked the cookie up. I was hungry, but I had no desire to eat. Still, I took a bite of the cookie. It tasted delicious, but as I chewed, the cookie was replaced with the harsh taste of iron. I was bleeding somewhere in my mouth.

What had happened the previous day never went away through the night—I dreamed it and relived it again, and when I woke up, I continued to think about it even though I didn't want to. I went over how it was just me and Lucky, then those three goons with Blond in front, looking sick with hate. I went over being attacked, the sound of flesh hitting flesh as they beat Lucky, the sound of my clothes ripping. As I changed out of my pajamas and into my bathrobe, I remembered the complete sense of helplessness and realized that it was the way I felt all the time. I had no control over my life. I was still a kid, but worse, my gender and race rendered me helpless around people like the drugstore proprietor, the men on the bus, and even the woman who first gave me a ride to see Lucky all those days ago. In my own life, I felt useless, ineffectual, and the feeling made me sick. I needed to wash.

I went to the shower and bathed. There was a little more blood that collected in a feminine napkin, but not much. Peeing was not too bad. The shower was both painful and pleasurable. Why hadn't I showered before? I felt cleansed.

After I dressed, my mother came into my room. "You should probably get on that bike today. You don't want to become afraid of riding it." She was sitting in front of my vanity, looking at herself in the mirror.

"I'm not afraid. I'm just not feeling so hot."

"Your face?"

"I have a headache. I think I'll stay around today. Do some summer reading."

"Nella, you are an enigma, I swear."

I shrugged. She started fidgeting with her hair, but I knew she wasn't studying her hair. I could see her looking at me in the mirror. I avoided her eyes.

"You can tell me anything, Nella, you know that, right?"

"You said that yesterday."

"You're being smart. And you're keeping something from me."

"I just have a headache, that's all."

"I'm sure you do. Look"—she stood and turned to me—"I don't know where you've been going or what you've been doing, but it's going to find your ass out if it hasn't already."

"Mama, please."

"Why don't you and I go for a walk today?"

I didn't answer her right away, but I told her I would go with her later. I told her, again, that I was not feeling well.

My mother wore her white gloves, so I did, too. She wore blue pumps and a pleated skirt suit. She had a navy capulet hat to match her suit, and the close-knit veil made it hard to read her face. She walked at a stately pace, and I must have looked like an idiot trying to keep up with her, with my white satin gloves and saddle shoes. I wore a hat, too, but one with a wide brim to help cover the bruises up.

She and I had no destination, but we walked determinedly. That is, she did. I followed. She would stop purposefully in front of a display window and look in. I would stand beside her. She would ask me a question and I'd give her a one-word answer.

"Thought about going to Milwaukee?" she'd ask.

"Yes," I'd say.

"Think you be going?"

"Maybe."

"Ran into any of the other colored kids?"

"No."

"Lonely here?"

"Yes."

"You fall on this street?"

"No."

"Nella, where did you go last night?"

"Around."

We didn't look at each other when we talked. We looked into the windows and sometimes I saw her reflection. I'm sure she saw mine, too.

That night, I ate very little dinner and kept to my one-word answers. Whenever someone would touch me, I'd flinch. I'd draw away and hold closer to my chair if I was sat or to the floor if I stood. I tried not to react, but I did. I did not want to be touched.

About a week later, my face was starting to look human again. Most of the puffiness went away, and I felt comfortable being out without covering up. I went out and rode my bike all over our little town, through each block up and down the streets. I missed Lucky, but I wasn't about to go see him. I was beginning to think of our relationship as over, but I ran into his sister while on one of my aimless trips throughout the town.

If it was not for her truck, filling out the entire lane on her side of the street and smelling heavily of diesel, I would not have noticed her. It was a farming community, sure, but it was unusual to see something so old there in town. Automobiles were scarce, and when they were around, they were at least from the 1940s. Lucky's sister's truck had to have had its heyday before the Second World War.

I heard her truck and looked over my shoulder. She drove slowly, but loudly, behind me. She was imposing without trying to be. I merged onto the sidewalk and stopped to let her pass. She smiled at me as she drove by, and the smile looked forced and uncomfortable on her face. She nodded, I think—it could be that her head only jerked in the bumpy truck. Then she sped away.

Seeing her was so unnerving that I biked home as soon as I lost sight of her truck. But I saw her again, days later. I heard her well beforehand, the breathy sighing and grumbling of the International's engine. Hearing it made me bike slower. And when I heard the engine stop—she had parked the truck somewhere—I stopped, too. It was three days after our first encounter, and I was not prepared to see her even after that brief warning. I thought that I could bike home, which was behind me, as fast as I could, but I knew that I wasn't going anywhere. I was shaking with fear and worry and could not bike if I wanted to (and I did want to). Instead of doing anything at all, I sat there on my bike. Greta, eventually, rounded the corner. I noted that she looked no less intimidating outside of her truck than in it.

As she got closer, she smiled her awkward smile again. I smiled back, and I'm sure it looked as genuine as it felt, which was not at all. She said, "Nella, don't be afraid." I shook my head once to show that I didn't understand her and that I was not afraid. She reached her hand out before she was close enough to shake mine. She wore no glove, so I could see that her large hand was rough and the nails kept short. It was not exactly clean. When she was near enough, I shook her hand.

"I'm Greta."

"I know. How is Lucky?"

"He's fine." Her smile went away when she talked, and it looked as if each word was exaggerated. "He's had worse days. You know, when he was a kid."

"Uh-huh," I said, though I didn't know what she was talking about. I remembered then, though, that she had broken his leg.

"Nella, it's been a couple of weeks."

"I know."

"Lucky and I were wondering."

My eyes filled with tears quickly. Before I spoke again, one drop fell. "I'm a couple of days late, but I'll wait."

"We can see somebody, or I can do it."

I was shaking my head before she finished. "That's how young girls die."

"But young animals don't. I've performed them lots of times on cattle and once on a horse."

"Forgive me, Miss Greta, but I ain't a cow."

"Of course, you aren't! That's not what I was saying. Please forgive me, Nella. Did you tell your mother?"

"No, no, we can't talk here. We can't talk at all."

"Lucky's worried sick."

"I can imagine. I should go home now."

"Lucky wants to see you. What should I tell him?"

"I don't know. I should go home."

"Wait. What will you do if it doesn't come?"

I didn't want her to ask me that. I got on my bike and pretended I didn't hear her, but she persisted and asked again. I rode a little away from her. "I don't know," I said.

"If you need help, please contact us."

I continued riding away, hoping that I was not pregnant, hoping I would really fall on my bike just in case I was. I was late, I knew, but I really didn't know how late. I didn't keep a calendar because, prior to the incident, I had no worries of periods missed or otherwise.

In the next week, which was three weeks after the encounter with Blond and pals, I missed Lucky to the point of aching. I was missing, too, my period. To do something about both, I rode my bike all over town in my pattern throughout the blocks and one-way signs. I heard the distinctive puttering of Greta's old truck. I picked up speed and followed the noise and the smell of exhaust (but it was a farm community, so it was hard not to smell

diesel everywhere). After about five minutes of searching, I found her. She waved as she usually did whenever
she saw me in town. And unusual for me, I waved back.
I then waved her over.

Greta held up a finger, telling me to wait. She then
looked around the streets intently, and when she found
a spot, she parked her colossus near a corner on one of
the streets off Main. I watched her from beside my bike,
shaking with nerves. I was only a little worried about
Greta, but I was very worried about who would see us
together.

She said my name as she drew nearer. I asked her,
quickly and quietly, to meet me half a mile outside of
town, next to one of the few trees along the road. She understood where with very little direction. I got back on
my bike and pedaled away, toward the spot where we
had planned to meet. She kept walking, trying to look as
if we were only passing each other.

It was dusty that day, and as I rode my bike to meet
Greta, I was assaulted with grit in my teeth and eyes. But
I rode fast and I tried to enjoy myself, listening to the
wind I made, the dirt on the spokes, the rubber on the
road, and my steady breathing. When I made it to the
tree and stopped, I tried to remain completely still, listening and feeling for a baby that may be growing inside
of me. I felt nothing. The blood racing through my head
from the energy I exerted biking there was loud enough
to drown out other sounds. It made me feel empty. Maybe,
I thought, I wasn't pregnant.

Soon, I could hear Greta's truck coursing through the
dirt road. I tensed up a little, but I was more relaxed than
I was in town. I was actually happy to have her to talk to.
In spite of the circumstances of when we first met, and

the reason of our meeting now, I could honestly say that I liked Greta. She had a calm demeanor, and she tended to settle the world around her. I thought back to that day when Lucky and I were attacked and how, when Greta had come along, everything had made more sense.

I saw the billows of dust her International made before I saw the truck itself. I dismounted and leaned my bike against the tree. Greta parked, opened her door, and jumped out. Although she was a big woman—not fat, just solid—she was agile.

"Nella," she said, speaking as she walked toward me. "Those bruises are gone and that beauty is coming through."

"Yeah, the bruises are mostly gone."

She stood in front of me and looked me over. "Yes, I see there's still some discoloration, but you do look a lot better. It's no mystery, you know, why Lucky is crazy about you. But that's just your looks, right?"

I nodded.

"Get your period?"

"No more pleasantries, huh? No, I didn't get it yet. I'm not sure when it's supposed to come, but it should have been here by now."

"If you want to get rid of it and you're sure you've got one in you, I can get it out in about twenty minutes. Half an hour at the most. I've done it before on cows for friends who were afraid that their heifers couldn't make it."

"Shoot, Greta, I don't want to talk about that."

"So, what do you want to do?"

"Let's talk about Lucky first. Is he doing all right?"

"Lucky is fine. He's working in his garage as usual, and he still helps me around the farm. He's looking better, too. He was sore for a while, but I'm sure he is okay. You know men—they won't tell you nothing. He misses you, though. I learned about you through him."

"Hm."

"You going to see him?"

"I don't know. My parents, you know."

"But you've seen him before. Is it that you'll get memories? At the garage."

I looked away from her. "I have to forget it to remember it. I'm not worried about the memories."

"You haven't told your parents anything yet."

"I've thought about it."

"You have to do something soon."

"I know. I asked you to meet me because I want you to be there when I do."

"As they say, there's no time like the present."

"Greta, I need to build up to this. I'm not you. I need a pleasant walk-in to something horrible."

"Let's sit. Let's go to my truck and sit."

Greta and I walked to the back of her old pickup truck. She let down the tailgate and we hopped into the bed and sat. We looked out onto the prairie. Heat devils played in the dirt before us, and Russian sage crept up here and there in purple clumps.

Eventually, Greta spoke. "You'll be wanting to keep it for what?"

"The baby? You mean if I'm pregnant?"

"Yes."

I didn't look at her. I didn't have an answer.

"There's no way it's Lucky's, at least that's what he tells me," she said.

I nodded.

"And I'm sure you don't care to see the men who did this to you again, do you?"

I shook my head no.

"Then why keep it?"

"I'm not a killer."

"It has to be alive to kill. It ain't took its first breath yet, so no worries there."

"I think that I'm more afraid of dying myself. If there was a sure way that I'll be alive when it's done and over, I'd be really considering. But I'm not ready to die, ma'am."

"I haven't killed a cow yet."

"I'm not a cow, Greta."

"It's really hard for me to talk to anyone, but it's harder when you won't even look at me."

I looked up at Greta, who sat next to me, and found I had to crane my neck to look at her face fully. In it, I saw Lucky—the lines his smiles and frowns had formed, the bone structure, the blue eyes. I shook my head at her. "You're a female Lucky."

"We look more like my father than my mother. You know they're both deceased now."

"Yes."

"Do you want me to go with you when you talk to your parents?"

"No transitioning into that, huh, Greta? All business."

"It's not business. You act like I'm dealing with farm animals or something."

"But you are, aren't you? I mean, you're acting in that way."

"I suppose there ain't no sense in wasting time. Get it done. And do it quickly."

"Yes, I would like you there. I don't know if I want Lucky there or not. When should we do it?"

"Your mother home now?"

I sighed. "I'd like to see Lucky first, I think. Just for a minute. Only a minute."

"Get your bike." Greta jumped off the gate. The truck bounced up a few inches taller. "We'll stop in on Janus, then we'll go talk to your mom."

The garage looked different. It was mostly the same, but I saw some changes. The grass was kept shorter. There was a sign on the door that assured visitors that the shop was open, but to please knock for admittance. The overhead doors were closed. "I'll wait out here," Greta said.

"How long should I be?"

"As long as you need to be." Greta leaned back in her seat and weaved her hands behind her head. "I ain't going nowhere but here."

I left her truck and walked to the garage. My stomach rumbled with both hunger and apprehension. I knew what I wanted to do today, and in preparation, I forgot to eat enough. Also, I did want to see Lucky, but I knew seeing him would kick up a lot of what happened from the dust, and I didn't want that. Thinking of what happened that day was almost enough to make me turn around and go back to the truck, or, better yet, get my bike off the truck and go home alone. But I went on, of course. I tried the door just to see if I really had to knock. The door was locked. This was Lucky fighting back, or preventing another attack.

The other thing the locked door did was make me work harder to see him. Walking up and opening a door was one thing, but having to knock was something else. It was boldly announcing my arrival. It was also asking for permission to come in. I thought back to that first day I went to visit Lucky and how I had watched him before he even knew I was there. In the time I had before he noticed me—before I had made myself known—I could compose myself and what I would say. Now, I had to knock and perform immediately. I hesitated. I looked back at Greta. She was still sitting with her head resting on her hands. Her eyes, I imagined, were closed. She was not looking at me.

I knocked and waited. I heard the wheels of Lucky's chair roll across his floor. I expected the door to open immediately, but instead, Lucky spoke. "Who is there?"

"Lucky, it's me."

"Nella." He opened the door quickly. "Nella, it's so good to see you."

"It's only for a minute."

"Can you come in for that minute?"

I stepped over the threshold. I looked into the shop before looking at Lucky. The garage was gated off with only a doorway for someone to go in and out of. The other area of the garage, where he made his sales and conducted business, was also gated off. There was now a counter where he could sit safely behind to take money and talk to customers. It wasn't a fort, but it was more guarded than his old setup.

"I hope it was just a one-time incident," I said.

"I'm sure it was, but I talked to an insurance agent, and he thought it best for liability reasons. You know, kids getting in the garage and whatnot."

"Sure."

"You look really good, Nell. Did you ride your bike all the way out here?"

"Your sister's outside. She drove me here."

"Are you meeting her in secret now?"

"What?"

He smirked.

"Lucky, can we sit somewhere?"

"I am sitting."

"Shut up."

"Sorry, Nella, come in."

I followed Lucky down the hall into his office. When we got there, I sat in a chair that was there for customers and he stayed in his wheelchair. I could see a few of the spokes were repaired in the wheels of his chair and that some of the wicker was missing from the back. "They got to my chair a little," he said.

"Guess I'm staring."

"I'm staring at you, too. It looks like you're healing well. How you feeling?"

"Fine, I guess. I'm here to see you, of course."

"Of course."

"But also, I have to tell you something."

"Are you breaking up with me? I mean, you haven't been by to see me in a while."

"It hasn't been easy. I think my parents are keeping a close eye on me."

"What did you tell them?"

I looked down in my lap. "I lied."

"You been living with that okay?"

I didn't look up. "I guess I've been kind of low lately. I can't forget what happened and I keep reseeing it in my head. I hear stuff around me, and I'm back there. The other day, my mother was sewing something. She cut the cloth, then ripped it apart. That sound was my shirt tearing. I was back in this garage. What about you?"

"I've been down, too. But I keep thinking about you." He rolled closer to me. "Nella, I was so worried that you—I don't know—a lot of things. I worried that you wouldn't see me again, that you'd hate me, that you'll move away, that you'll go a little soft in the head, that you're pregnant."

"Oh, Luck, I can never hate you, but I think I am pregnant."

"What?"

I looked up. "I think I'm late." Lucky's expression made me cry. His skin paled and his blues eyes had white all around them.

"Late?"

"Yes. I don't know exactly because I never really kept track. I never had to." I was sobbing as I talked.

"I know."

"I'm going to have to tell my parents the truth. About what happened that day, about why I was here that day, you know."

"You'll have to tell them about me."

"Yes."

"Greta has ways to—"

"I know. I'm repeating myself. I'm here . . ." I looked at him. I stopped sobbing enough to close my mouth and look at him. The familiarity of his face was comforting. I knew his cheekbones and how they rose and fell. I knew the narrowness of his cheeks, the pointiness of his chin. I knew his eyes so blue they were foreign to me, but friendly. "I'm here to say that I do care about you. I may even love you. I came to say that I am happy I met you, Lucky."

"You're saying goodbye."

"Yes, I'm saying goodbye. I know that when I tell my mother what happened, I'll soon be in Milwaukee."

"Just like that."

"Yes."

His head jerked slightly. "It would be corny to say that in another time . . ."

"It would be. And useless."

Lucky's eyes teared up. "But," he said, "in another time . . . And you may be wrong. Maybe your parents will be more forgiving."

"I should go."

"If you are pregnant, what will you do with the baby?"

"I haven't thought that far yet."

Greta was sleeping when I returned to the truck and awoke only when I shut the door after me. "You're done? Were you gone long?"

I shook my head no.

"Look at you. You're even beautiful when you're crying."

That made me cry harder.

"Said goodbye to Lucky, I suppose. Goodbyes are hard, but they are a lot softer than you think. This is a homey analogy, but look at it this way: When you plant a seed, it's like saying goodbye. You think you'll never see the seed again because you're covering it up with dirt. It's like you're burying it, right? But you'll see it again."

"It would have changed," I said. "It's not the same seed anymore."

"No, but nothing ever is." Greta sat up fully and started the engine. "Do you know what you'll say to your parents?"

"My mother. I cannot tell my father. I have a general idea."

"Do you want me to tell her?"

"No, I think that would be worse. I just want you there."

She put the truck into gear and pulled away. We drove away toward Kismet. We didn't talk. I stared out at the fields and random houses that grew on the prairie. Why did I want Greta there? Maybe it was because I knew that my mother wouldn't kill me with a witness there. Maybe it was because Greta brought common sense to wherever she was. I felt that if she just stood there as I told about what happened and what I now feared, I would be able to get the words out. My mother would listen without interrupting. Greta could mediate. I don't know what I wanted.

"Was Lucky okay when you left him?" Greta asked, breaking me out of my thoughts.

"He was a little broken up. I felt bad, too, but I know my mother won't let me see him again."

Greta made a noise in her throat that worked its way into a light laugh.

"He talks about you all the time. More than any other girl before you. But remember what I told you about the seed. It's hokey, I know, but there's truth in it." The day's sun was growing stale and the light was changing outside. Shadows played behind brush and tumbleweeds, falling silos, and farmhouses. Soon, the houses were closer together and more modern. We could see people dodging the truck as we drove by, and traffic picked up a bit. I directed Greta to turn down Main Street, a right here and a left there. Although it was warm, I was cooling down. I shivered. My knees knocked and my teeth chattered. We were coming upon my house. And I was cold.

Greta and I sat on the couch, and my mother was on her velvet-covered Queen Anne chair before us. She looked at Greta as I explained what had happened and what may happen, but every so often, she would look at me. Her nostrils seemed to take up most of her face. Her large lips puckered out in a moue. Her chest evenly rose and settled throughout. She spoke not a word. When I finished telling her about the attack and my potential pregnancy, she remained silent. I could hear her breathing, which came evenly and crisply. She wouldn't linger on a breath. Her punishment, I knew, would be given without argument. I knew I wouldn't see Lucky even accidentally anymore. I was leaving Kansas for good.

"You are here for what?" she finally said, and this was to Greta.

"I think it is because Nella wanted someone to defer to if she couldn't get the story out."

"Defer to."

Greta nodded.

"You are a grown woman, Miss Greta, and you knew this was going on? My daughter and your son—"

"Brother, ma'am."

"Well, brother then, your brother. You knew he and Greta were running around together?"

Greta shook her head. "No, ma'am. Not until the day of the incident."

"The day of. And why didn't you come to me and Nella's father the day of the incident?"

Greta looked at me, then back at my mother. "Nella asked me not to."

"You answer to Nella. You come when she wants you to and stay put when she doesn't want you around. You know a child—Miss Greta, Nella's only a child—has been attacked and you do nothing?"

"Forgive me, ma'am, but I did not know where Nella lived. I did not know how to find you or your husband. I wanted to, also, respect Nella's wishes."

"Respect Nella's wishes? She is only a child! She may be colored, but only a child nonetheless."

"I didn't think much of her color."

"That ain't neither here nor there, Miss Greta. Are you lying to me, too? Forgive me for getting too forward, but how did you two find each other this day?"

"I found her, Mama. I saw her around town a few times and got the courage to talk to her."

My mother stood. "What happened?" Just like that, she was hysterical. "My baby raped by a gang of white men. My only daughter. My only child."

I stood, too. "Mama."

"My God, what happened? And now you may be pregnant?" She was crying. I caught sight again of her chest moving up and down with each breath, this time faster. I saw how large her breasts were, how she was not only my mother but a woman, which sounds simple, but in light of what I had just told her—of my affair with Lucky and being taken by a bunch of strange men—her being a woman was significant. She looked helpless and I was helpless. And Greta, too, had nothing to do. We could do nothing. My mother stood there crying about a lost innocence that I'm not sure I ever had. I stood and swayed with her. Greta swayed. It was horrible, but nice. It was like being in church. It was all three of us throwing all hope to something outside of ourselves, hopefully greater than us three. Hopefully benevolent.

But my mother broke it up as quick as she started it, that shared experience of being helpless and having a power in knowing. "I'm going to have to ask you to leave, Miss Greta," she said. "Thank you for bringing my Nella home. Good luck to you and your brother."

Greta stood and nodded at us both. I wouldn't see her again for years.

When Greta left, I expected lots of words from my mother, but she was silent again. She went to her part of the house, which was her sewing nook, and I went to my part, which was my bedroom. I cried myself to sleep. I was mourning the loss of the relationship I had with Lucky, but I was also crying out of relief. My mother now knew.

When I was very young, I would wake up with my mother smiling down at me. Her fingers combed softly through my straightened hair. She smelled of coffee and bacon. She smelled like butter and everything wonderful. "Hey, my baby girl," she'd say. And I'd sit up and hug her, happy to be alive and happy to be hers.

It surprised me to see her over me the morning after I told her the truth. She was not smiling, but she wasn't frowning, either. Her fingers were combing through my hair, which was slightly tangled from sweating overnight. I smiled up at her. "Why didn't you have any other kids?"

"You were hard to come by. I was twenty-seven when I finally got pregnant, but we were trying since I was nineteen. Doctor said I couldn't have no more."

"I'm really sorry about everything."

"Your father comes home today."

"I know."

She continued to comb through my hair. Her expression didn't change. "If you're pregnant," she said, "I don't know what to do. I heard, long ago, that there are homes where young girls go in that way. They wait until they have the baby. The baby goes for adoption, and the girl goes back home."

"I could do that."

"You won't come back home, though. You'll be going to Milwaukee to live with your grandmother. I never thought I'd be saying this, but it's probably safer for you there."

"What will Daddy say?"

My mother took her hand from my head. She hummed in her way: deep alto with too much vibrato. She stood up and went to my dresser. I sat up and watched her fuss at her hair. Her lips were pressed together in a slight grin around her humming. Satisfied with the hairs tucked back into her bun, she stopped singing and said, "I'll have to tell him something else. That you and I decided Milwaukee would be better for you. Nella, do you know what I'm doing for you?"

"Yes, ma'am. If I'm not, you know, pregnant, do I still have to go to Milwaukee?"

"Yes. What can we do with you here?"

I lay back down in bed. I floated down. I had said goodbye to Lucky because I knew this would happen, but hearing it from my mother, and knowing the certainty of it, was something else.

My mother left me to get up. I didn't budge until I couldn't hold my bladder anymore. What I saw while on the toilet made me happy then upset again: blood. Strikingly dark scarlet blood on my white cotton panties. But why not before I found Greta? Before I said goodbye to Lucky?

I was angry for other reasons. Because of being attacked by strangers, because of hate, my life was being affected. Had those three men not come, Lucky and I would still be together. Maybe I'd still be going home to Milwaukee for school, but I'd be leaving for education, not fear.

I cleaned up and wondered how much would change, now that I'd gotten my period. Anything? Could I reason with my mother at all? When I finished, I went to find my mother, who was reading alone in the living room. I stood and watched her for a while. Even though she was in her favorite chair and reading a novel, she wasn't in complete repose. Lines wavered on her forehead and her lips were tight. She was still angry, but I couldn't care. "I ain't pregnant," I said.

"What?" She looked up at me, her face opening only slightly.

"I said I'm not pregnant. I'm menstruating."

She smiled and placed her book down. She stood up. "You feel normal?"

"What do you mean?"

"You don't . . ." She stopped, then found her words. ". . . feel any extra pain or anything?" Years later, I would realize that she was trying to find out if I'd miscarried.

"I don't feel any different than any other time."

"Honey, that's great. I'm so happy."

I sat down on the couch. She was happy, sure, but I wasn't there yet. "I'm glad I'm not pregnant, but I feel like I've lost lots of fights here, Mama."

"You won an important battle, baby."

"I lost Lucky. Not because of anything he or I did. He was a perfect gentleman, Mama. He was hurt that day, too. They hurt him bad."

My mother sat back down in her chair. "But he's white."

"I know what he is. He is white, but he cared for me. He was the only friend I had here."

"I tried to introduce you to Mrs. Taylor's and Mrs. Cox's daughters, but you were always traipsing around town, supposedly window-shopping and eating stuff from the grocery."

"And how many of your friends did you meet through your mother's friends when you were my age?"

"Nella, what do you want from me? Do you think I should let you have your rendezvous with a white man, especially after what happened to you? And what would your father say?"

"I didn't say that I wanted to keep going off with Lucky. I'm only saying that I don't have much choice here." I knew it didn't matter. Nothing I said was going to change anything. "I don't know what Daddy will say. But Lucky was my friend. Because of three hateful white men, we won't be friends anymore. I know I shouldn't have snuck around behind your and Daddy's back, but I also know I couldn't have brought him home to dinner. Lucky and I made it work in our way. And he never took advantage of me."

"I don't know how old that white man is," she said. "He has a garage! Nella, you are only sixteen."

"I turned seventeen a few months ago, Mama."

She stood up again and grabbed her book. "You are still a child. My child! When you grown and up out of my house, run around with who you want, but for now you do as I say." She made to leave the room, then turned back to me, pointed at me. "And even if your daddy and I were out of the picture, you'd still have to sneak around if you were dating a white man. Is that the kind of life you want?"

"Are you going to tell Daddy?"

She put her hand down and looked at me as if just now realizing that Daddy didn't know any of what was going on. We were in a staring contest, both of us heaving as if we'd just finished doing some heavy lifting. Then she said, "You haven't learned shit."

In bed that night, pushing toward the wee hours, my eyes were wide open. I marveled at how bright the room was in only moonlight. I imagined escaping, grabbing my bike and riding to Lucky to give him a proper goodbye. I wanted to have the courage to make that fantasy real, to go and find him and kiss him once again. But whatever courage I had had to make the relationship happen in the first place—and that was me who put it into action—was gone. I began to wonder if I loved Lucky or if I even liked him. Was it instead just the intrigue of doing something forbidden? Or was it just that Lucky liked me? He was the one who found beauty in me first; I had to search for beauty in him.

Years later, I would look back on the relationship I had with him as a little, quiet fight against the powers that be, one of many on the continuum of the fight for racial justice and equality. And we lost that fight. I wouldn't come to that conclusion until I was ready to see Lucky again, but he was already gone.

PART 3
1933

Margit Svoboda's hair, roughly blond, was stringy from lack of washing. She had it done up in a bun fastened with a Bakelite clip. I imagined it draped over her broad shoulders. I imagined being allowed to touch her hair. The thought of what it must feel like made me sweat.

One of her four children, the little boy, played absently with one of her fallen curls, his cheeks slightly sunken from hunger, his pallid thumb in his mouth. I so much wanted to be beside her, too, with an arm draped around her, sharing those kids with her. She'd turn to smile at me and I'd smile back. We'd rise together to sing the hymn. Our hands would rest on the pew in front of us, mine covering hers.

That was a ridiculous fantasy.

I had not been in a church for years, and the day I chose to go was hot. It was 1933, and one of many days tied together with heat, dust, and unblemished blue skies and clear nights. The closeness of the church, the tone of the choir and the coughs and the echoes resonating through the organ's pipes, the dry heat, and the sense of my own hypocrisy made me focus only on Margit sitting right in front of me. I wanted to touch her neck and trace the spaces between the freckles. I wanted to tug the curls that hung loosely down and spiraled into her shirt. If I sat a little farther forward, I could smell her.

The heat and Margit's beauty made it difficult for me to follow the rituals of church, so I followed Margit: When she stood, I stood. When she sat, I sat. And when she went up to the altar for Communion, I followed behind her and her children. When she stood, I noticed the build of her. Although she was a hefty, strong woman, her neck was long and thin. Stray curls, lighter blond than the stuff stacked on top of her head, lined the bottom of her hairline. The skin there looked fresh. I stood along with the rest of the congregation for the final prayer of the service, but instead of bowing my head, I stared at her bare neck, and as if she felt my eyes running over the tendons and the few freckles, she raised her hand and brought it back to cover her neck. She held it there for a short minute, and I could see that her fingernails were cut low and her skin red with work. I could see, too, the cheap band of gold plate on her ring finger. She then slid her hand away, as if wiping off sweat. I looked down at my feet and said the Lord's Prayer with everyone else.

When the service ended, I followed the crowd outside and waited my turn to talk to the pastor. I tried to keep the two things for which I needed to ask for forgiveness in my mind: my long absence from the church and my ruining Janus's leg. I thought of other sins I'd committed for which I needed to be forgiven: for loving Daddy a little too much; for masturbating in his study while wearing the burlap shirt I made for him out of seed sacks; for cursing Mama her sickness, which was probably more imagination than malady; for cursing Janus because I was responsible for him after Daddy died; for wishing that Mama, that anyone else, had died instead of Daddy; for wanting women. I should have been a Catholic, and then I could go anonymously share these sins with another and only be slightly admonished, lightly rebuked, and charged and sentenced prayers to Mary and God.

The pastor finally stood before me, in his robe and collar, looking benevolent and skeptical at once. I couldn't help but feel hotter looking at him wearing all that heavy black in the heat. He was a tall man, and he obviously tried to use his height, but I was a tall woman. He shook my hand, but he looked suspicious. "We've been missing you and the rest of the family, Miss Obeck," he said.

"I've been helping out on the farm," I told him.

"Not much to do there right now, is there?" the pastor asked me.

Of course there wasn't, as there was not on any farm in Seward County, but that didn't mean we didn't try. His comment, though, made me notice my shoes—work boots that were kind of hidden beneath my dress. "My father's dead," I said. He should know that.

"Ah, yes. I'm sorry about that. You were here for the funeral."

"That I was."

"That was about a year ago," he said. I didn't correct him. "But no one's died today, so what brings you?"

"I accidently clubbed my brother's leg. I didn't mean to do it, and he's hurt really bad. During the last roundup, he got caught up in the pen with the jackrabbits. I clubbed his leg pretty bad, so he's at home getting better. I thought that I'd ask Jesus for his forgiveness and that it'll get to him quicker if I came here to ask, instead of doing it at home."

"Hurt badly? Can he walk?" His attitude changed abruptly, and he seemed genuinely concerned in what I had to say.

"Not without help," I said. "He's mostly holed up in bed on doctor's orders."

"And how are you all getting along out there? You need any help?"

"In what way do you mean?" I skipped being polite. I was beyond the point of rejecting help after these many years of the Depression; I wouldn't even entertain the notion of turning down help of any kind. "We are kind of hungry."

"We are all kind of hungry, Greta. How about with the boy? Help him convalesce?"

I thought this quickly over. Who would come to my house? Would I be questioned for the boy's condition?

"I can do it," a woman said from behind me. I turned to see who had spoken and was met with that pile of blond hair, various shades of sun-tinted ash framing her face. Later that year, when Margit would leave me on the floor of the barn, crying for her, I would remember that as the moment I fell in love with her, standing there willingly in front of the church, but Janus would have told me that was the beauty of memories: they can act however you want them to. And instead of saying, *Yes, come over. Come now. Come often*, I asked, "What can you do to help, exactly?"

Her voice was as strong as mine, but she spoke with more confidence than I could ever muster. "I can help bathe the boy. Lord knows I've lots of experience with that. I can wash clothes, if you need it, cook, clean. And, of course, I can help with the boy overall. Get him moving."

"I don't have any money," I said. I regretted saying it immediately: it was a useless comment to make.

"Pay me in kindness. God will find a way to compensate us all when this drought ends."

The day before I broke Janus's leg, I held Daddy's hunting rifle like a marksman and aimed at jackrabbits, one at a time. Knocked them off easily. They hopped slowly up the hill, toward the little wheat and corn that survived. They came tirelessly, hungrily, attempting anything. Before each shot I aimed, inhaled, exhaled slightly, and held my breath, and then I quietly pulled the trigger, just as Daddy taught me. Janus yelped happily with each report.

With the emptiness of western Kansas, there was nothing around to stop the sound of that bullet leaving the barrel. It reverberated against the cloudless sky each time, ripping through the silence. The shots were deafening, but they cleared the head and made it possible to hear that there was nothing there taller than us and stuff we grew for acres. That quiet made me feel safe, even when nothing would grow.

The rabbits leaped in erratic ways when they were hit. They went down fast. And though it seemed cruel, the killing of jackrabbits was humane. It was euthanasia. Those rabbits were better off dying instead of starving. Better for them to die quickly. I'd shoot and they would leap their last leap, then fall to the ground without a sound. Or some were noisy, dying with a cry reminiscent of a hurt baby.

And the ones who weren't shot yet were juggernauts for our plants—they kept coming. I kept shooting.

Whenever Janus was home, he'd follow me everywhere, sometimes asking questions about the things I did around the farm, but mostly he was quiet because I was quiet. Sometimes he'd read to me from his dime-store novels or from magazines. When he could get them from Reb Roberts, who owned the local garage in Seward, he'd read owner's manuals to cars or passenger car shop manuals. He would read about the engine and the parts of the cars and trucks. Sometimes, he'd tinker around in Daddy's old 1920 Model T, which I let him do because we weren't running it anymore.

Mostly Janus just followed me. He mimicked the way I walked and acted. When Daddy was still around, it was him who Janus emulated and admired, but now that he was dead and Mama was completely despondent, the boy depended on me. Although he was twelve, he wanted me to tuck him in at night. I didn't feel comfortable doing it, but I did. Then I would pat his shin before turning his light off. Awkwardly, he'd wrap his arms around my waist whenever he was really excited about something, but those moments were rare.

I was Janus's exemplary adult. I hardly talked. It's not that I didn't want to talk to Janus; it's just that I couldn't think of what to say. I didn't have much to say to anybody. And because I was a quiet example, Janus hardly talked. When he became a man, I was always amused at how much he did talk—a mile a minute, and every word as important as the last one. He would become a joker and someone who would love his women completely. When I look back on it, I don't know if I could recognize those elements in him then.

Janus's attachment and loyalty were very pet-like. I tried not to, but I compared him to a dog, specifically Trunk, the dog Daddy killed back when the Depression first got to be too much for our family.

"Kill her or starve her," Daddy said. He took the dog out back. Whistled and the hungry dog followed. I followed, too. "You sure you want to see this?" he asked.

I said nothing. I only looked up at him and tried to make my face as plain as the moon.

We walked to the edge of the yard, right near the wheat. Trunk had enough energy to wag her tail, which nearly moved me to tears. Daddy stopped. Trunk and I stopped, too.

"You stay here, girl," Daddy said. I wasn't sure if he meant me or the dog until he tapped my shoulder for me to join him.

We walked away a few feet, and when he stopped, I stopped. Then he turned to the dog. Trunk's rib cage showed through her coat. Her thick fur had lost its sheen months ago. A fly buzzed around her eye, and Trunk was so dejected that she didn't bite at it.

"We're doing this because we care for you, dog," Daddy said.

"Her name's Trunk," I reminded him. I didn't feel out of place doing so.

"Trunk," he said.

The dog didn't act differently when she heard her name. She did not perk up or respond in any way. Daddy raised the gun, and although Trunk had hunted with her master many times before, she didn't flinch when he pointed the barrel at her. I took a small step toward Trunk, not sure what it was I was doing.

"You sure you want to see this?" he asked again.

I breathed in, regretting it immediately because of the dust on the wind. I nodded my head. Daddy pulled the trigger and the dog slumped over immediately, too wasted to fight. I didn't blame my father; he was Trunk's savior. And that's how I saw myself, a savior for those suffering rabbits.

"There," Janus said now, breaking my reverie. He pointed to a jackrabbit slowly hopping toward us. I looked at the heft of Janus's arm and remembered why I was thinking about Trunk in the first place. My stomach jumped. I swallowed and raised the rifle. Aim. Inhale. Exhale a little and hold breath. Shoot.

Soon, I shot my seventeenth and last rabbit of the day. Janus cheered me good-naturedly. It occurred to me then that I probably had not had a real conversation with him ever. I looked at him and wondered if he was small for his age. "Do you think Mama has food ready?" I asked.

"Suppose so," he answered.

"Hungry?" I asked.

He nodded. He had a goofy, shy grin on his face. My heart went out to him because he was so desperate for someone, even for me. Instead of talking, I nodded back at him and then pointed my head toward our house. I started home. He followed me.

Biscuits with flour-and-water gravy were set out on the table, waiting for us. Our mother, who worked like shoe elves, was already back in bed. I grabbed the washbasin and took it back outside to the water pump. As I pumped the handle, I imagined Mama cooking, her thick ankles covered with Daddy's old wool socks, her stocky body moving about the kitchen. Mama kneading the bread with her huge hands, white knuckled and marred with shiny scars from years gone by. She would do this with a hush filled with hurry. Then when the biscuits were done and the gravy made with old grease, flour, and water was finished, she'd set the table: a place for each of her kids, for her dead husband, and for herself. Then she'd sit at the table and eat her share—the smallest share to only quiet her hunger enough. Or maybe she ate a king's portion. Somehow, her ankles stayed thick. She'd eat quick and alone, leaving almost no crumb, no gravy residue for her son or daughter to see. Then she'd rush back to bed.

"Something's got to give," I said. No one was around to hear, which was good: I didn't want to explain what that something was. I wondered if she was keeping meat or good vegetables for herself; she kept that weight some-how. Maybe she hated us. Maybe she wanted us to go into the woods with only biscuit crumbs to mark our way. But this was the prairie, so there were no woods. That was the hunger talking, I told myself, but I couldn't shake the feeling that Mama wanted us gone.

The basin was overfull. I took it back to the house.

"Come get cleaned, Jan," I called.

My little brother half skipped to me, pulling his shirt off along the way. I saw the definition of his ribs but tried not to look. The basin of water was covered with a skin of dust, but my brother and I still scrubbed our faces and hands in the water. Washing was pleasant. I wet my hair along the hairline to cool off and advised Janus to do the same.

When we entered the house, both times for me, we did not say anything to our mother. She said nothing to us. We sat down to dinner without her, as usual. On that day, I thought that I should say grace because I wanted to teach the boy something besides shooting rabbits and tending crops that were not there. "Let's bow our heads," I said.

Janus looked up at me, not smiling. "We're going to pray?"

"Yes. We should."

He didn't put his head down yet, but looked at me skeptically. "You know any prayers for grace?"

I didn't answer. "Bow your head, boy."

He bowed. And so did I. I felt silly, looking down at my plate of biscuits and greasy flour gravy, made with grease from some meat cooked so long ago that it had lost all its semblance of the animal it came from. The gravy had congealed a little, so I knew that Mama had cooked more than a little while ago. *This can't be it*, I thought, but I would not be able to define what *it* was if someone asked me to. Was it the food I was feeling desponded about? Or was it our mother's reclusiveness?

"Okay," I said.

He raised his head and looked at me.

"It was a silent prayer," I said.

Janus and I ate the bread as if it were gourmet goodness. We were famished, but even after eating, we were still wanting. Neither one of us mentioned our enduring hunger. We only looked at each other knowing our need. If I knew then what would happen, I would have told him, *Tomorrow, I'll destroy your leg. You will be maimed for life.*

The next day was another day of full sun, and maybe over one hundred degrees by midmorning. Though it was Sunday, I wore boots because I didn't want to get trampled by farmers or rabbits. Janus went barefoot, though I warned him against it. "When the clubbing starts," I told him, "I want you to stay back."

"I think I'm old enough to join in. Other boys from school do."

"You ain't other boys."

We walked toward the meet-up place as we talked. I could already hear the sounds of the other farmers who remained on the prairie and their sons preparing for the roundup. We were soon in the midst of a crowd of men and boys. Each person bore a heavy stick of some type: big tree branches, baseball bats, billy clubs, and broken broomsticks. Anything you could think of, people held by the hilt. As usual, I was one of a small few women in the crowd waiting to round the pests up. The other women, wives and daughters, walked a little ways from us, preparing to sit near enough to watch the roundup but far enough away to be safe. Some of them had young kids with them. "You should go join them," I told Janus, nodding at the women.

"What? With all those women?" he said.

"I'm a woman. Look, there are kids there, too."

"Why can't I be a part of the roundup, Greta?"

When we reached the grounds, most of the women ended up on the side away from the roundup area, some holding umbrellas up, some with hats on. Those who were to participate in the roundup congregated in a loose crowd. I overheard farmers talking about what wouldn't grow and what couldn't be fed. It was the same talk every Sunday. Some of the men nodded at me and I nodded back, but mostly I was paying attention to Janus, trying to get him out of the impending fray. I think Peter Svoboda, one of the organizers, was watching me and Janus, because when I finally got him to go on the sidelines with the women and little children, Peter whistled a piercing screech. The crowd started and almost immediately went quiet. We lined up, forming a wall, and banged our clubs on the ground. Whenever we saw rabbits, we'd corral them into a large pen that was raised just for that jackrabbit roundup. When it was all over, the pen was usually destroyed.

There was a level of adrenaline I felt during the jackrabbit roundups that was unique for me. I have hunted, I have danced, but almost nothing was like the energy and excitement I felt when gathering those pests up, then clubbing them to death. The closest experience I had that made me feel that way, as of yet, was the day when Daddy went a little too far with me. He had found me in the barn one night after drinking at someone else's farm.

I was seeing to the milk cow (who, like Daddy, was long gone from this world) before turning in when he came in. I greeted him and he said nothing. Soon, though, I felt him behind me, embracing me, rocking me in his arms as I've watched him rock Mama so many times before. He smelled like moonshine and moved as if he were filled with it. Uncomfortable, but aroused, I moved away from him. He pulled me closer.

"Oh, Greta," he said, his lips right against my ear. I felt him grow through my skirts, his pants, and I shivered with it. Even at that point, I knew that I didn't care for men, but something about all of it made me respond to him as he wanted me to. But I was repulsed, too, not only because he was a man, but because he was my father. I felt loved but desired only as a whore, which made the incident that much more arousing in a way I still cannot explain. And when he started to kiss my neck, taking the curls from the nape between his lips, I had begun to cry. I felt at once pleasure and revulsion, an immense love for him and a hate like I'd never felt before.

Roundups gave me mixed feelings, too. I believed that we were doing something to save our farms, I thought that we were saving our way of life, but this didn't stop the oppressive guilt I felt from killing animals we would not eat for fear of illness. Those rabbits were defenseless, and like us, they were just trying to live longer in spite of the drought. I'm sure others felt that guilt like me; when Black Sunday came in April, some of us believed it was the Second Coming because of what we did to those jackrabbits. At every roundup, we got the rabbits in the pen and closed the gate. We then went after them, clubbing rabbits like so many bad dreams. The jackrabbits' screams and our clubs pounding against dirt and fur that concealed very little fat made a horrible noise. And all I could see was blood and fur flying created by us, a frenzy of farmers determined to keep what little crops we had.

On the day I hurt Janus, we had penned many of them up in an oblong rectangle with enough room for the farmers and hundreds of jackrabbits. You'd find a rabbit and get something that mattered first—the head, the spine. Then you'd whack at that rabbit to still it. Beat it until it didn't move. I was always hesitant with the first one, and it seemed the first rabbit screamed the loudest, but as time wore on, I became methodical in my killing. Swift. My mind would clear itself of all thought. I saw the fur and blood, but the scene before me was out of focus, fuzzy with the work of killing. The jackrabbit's long ears would sometimes catch my eye, but mostly I *saw* nothing.

Like any chore, you could find your rhythm and the actions became meditative. However, there was that underlying guilt that ebbed and grew in spite of the peacefulness that was there. That feeling would grow intense until the last rabbit was killed, and afterward, I only had contrition.

The day I hurt Janus was no different. There were a lot more rabbits, but everything was how we expected it. By the tenth or twelfth rabbit, I heard something too child-like. Someone yelled, "Stop!" but I kept beating. Then someone caught my arm. Not understanding, I tried to continue to kill my rabbit, but the resistance against my arm was strong. I blinked, and then I understood: I was being stopped. A skinny but strong kid, near Janus in age, held my arm. He was screaming, but I didn't hear him. I looked down at my rabbit and saw Janus. It could not be Janus. It was as if a hypnotist had snapped his fingers at me. "Stop," the boy said again. I shook my head. "Your brother," he said.

Something in my stomach dropped. I burped up bile then swallowed it down quickly. Did Janus follow me here? I panicked: I looked left. I looked right. The other boy stepped aside, and there, sure enough, lay Janus, his face streaked with mud and blood. I prayed it was rabbit's blood. He had been crying. His leg lay awkwardly away from his body, obviously broken. "Janus," I said. I dove down to him and tried to pick him up. He screamed out, and since I was close to him then, I heard him. Overwhelming grief shook me. I cried. All around us, the men and boys were still clubbing, unaware of my brother.

"I can help you," the kid said. He put his club down and came closer to us. I then recognized him: the Svoboda kid. Carefully, the boy and I tried lifting Janus, but Janus cried out again. "Let's use the clubs," the boy said. He was strong and capable, and I was thankful for him. He moved easily around Janus, in spite of the chaos of the roundup.

We placed the longest club behind Janus's shoulders and had him hold on. I gripped the club's ends and, carefully, the Svoboda boy lifted Janus's legs. We walked slowly with him, the crowd clearing around us as we came through. Someone must have sent word, because when we got home, the doctor was there to meet us.

And days later, it would become too much for me to handle—Janus and Mama and the farm—so I would go to church. And later yet, Margit would come to help. When Margit first arrived to help at our house, she brought her daughter, Ruth, with her. I wasn't expecting that. Ruth seemed a little tired, especially for a child. She had to be about thirteen or fourteen years old. She wasn't nearly as pretty as her mother. Her dark brown hair was cut just below her ears, and it had no shine to it. The sun highlighted only grays in her hair, which probably was her brown hair covered with dust, but the whole effect made her look like a dumb, dowdy old woman. She was too thin and straight; her knees knobbed inward awkwardly beneath the hem of a dress that might have fit her last year. She also had acne and greasy skin, which I couldn't understand because of the dryness. I hardly remembered seeing her from church. She must have sat a little apart from the rest of the family. Or she may be forgettable.

"You remember Ruth?" Margit announced, proud but apologetic. "She'll help me for the first couple of days. Hope you don't mind."

"Not at all," I said.

Mama, who had recently taken to shuffling around the house since I hurt Janus, sniffled and scratched the back of her throat loudly.

"And here is Mother."

"Hello again, Mrs. Obeck," Margit said. Mama shuffled away.

"Please don't mind her," I said. "I can show you around, if you'd like that."

Margit agreed to the tour. She and Ruth followed me as I showed them the outside of the bedrooms and the inside of the other rooms. Poor Janus was sleeping in his room, his leg suspended above the bed by some contraption the doctor had brought over so that it may heal uninterrupted. He woke when we entered and sat up the best he could. He was very polite when I introduced him to Margit and Ruth, but he wasn't enthused about it. Margit smiled the whole time during the tour and sometimes jotted things down in a little notebook she kept on hand. Ruth didn't react at all. I kept expecting her to ask Margit to pick her up, though I knew the girl was in her early teens. She just seemed so needy and dependent on Margit. Even as he lay there with a broken leg, Janus was much more animated than Ruth.

After the tour, we three sat down at the kitchen table, Margit with her little pad and pencil. "What is the most important thing you need to get started?" Margit asked me.

"Before Janus was hurt," I said, "he was responsible for keeping the place tidy. Since he's been hurt, well . . ." I motioned around me at the growing mess. "I have to take care of the farm, you understand?"

"Yes, I do." She wrote in her notebook, but she also leaned in closer. "And your mother?"

"She's been moving around more since Janus was hurt, but only to get more in the way. This place is a mess, ain't it?"

Margit said, "We'll start by straightening up. It may be the only thing we do today. When was the last time you bathed him?"

"Oh, I didn't. I couldn't. He washed before he was hurt. And the doctor said not to get his leg wet. I think it's been about a week and a half since he had his last bath. That was before the roundup."

"Okay. I can give him a washing tomorrow. And you, would you be wanting a bath?"

"I'm fine bathing myself." I probably answered too quickly. My face felt suddenly flushed.

She gave an embarrassed, tight smile. "Have you been bathing yourself, I mean? Are you taking care of yourself, Greta? And your mother, while we're at it."

"I draw her a bath once a week or so."

"We can help with that if you need it."

"How long will you be here helping me?"

"Today or overall? Today, we're going to get at least the bedrooms and the kitchen clean. Then we're going to come until your brother gets better."

"You are an angel." I felt undeserving.

"Oh, I wouldn't go as far as that." She stood up and Ruth stood, too, watching her mother for cues. "We should get started right away," Margit said. To her daughter, she said, "Go get the cleaning bucket out of the truck. Make sure everything is in it before you bring it inside."

Without a word, Ruth left us, her head held down. Margit began by moving the chairs to a corner of the kitchen. Then grabbing the broom, she began to sweep. When Ruth returned, Margit had her empty the cleaning supplies onto the kitchen table, and then she took the bucket and went out the back. I walked over to the sink to look out the window above it, and from there watched her walk to the water pump. She took hold of the handle of the pump and quickly forced water into her bucket. And I watched her return.

I stayed with Margit and Ruth for only a few minutes more and saw in that little time their efficiency and abilities. Then I left the house and went to work in the fields. There really wasn't anything to do outside but dodge dust. The Dust Bowl, as it was called later, had left the soil loose and dry. The farm was completely useless. The few plants we had were greatly compromised. I wasn't going to do anything out there but think. Maybe masturbate. I got in the tractor and drove it through the fields to a place I knew no one could see me. When I got there, I parked and jumped out of the tractor. I rested against one of the wheels and found myself crying uselessly. I didn't know exactly why I cried, but I knew it had something to do with the guilt I felt for Janus's leg and for having Margit Svoboda come clean my house when I was perfectly capable. It was nice, though, to have Margit over. It was wonderful to see her and that blond hair piled atop her head. I thought of her and everything went cloudy. A new kind of shame started to come in.

Eventually, I quit my spot in the field. I felt conflicted about what I wanted when I returned: the Svobodas still there or the Svobodas to be gone for the day. I found that they were just finishing up, and I was fine with that. We went over what we both expected for the next day, and then Ruth and Margit were ready to leave. When they were at the door, I grabbed Ruth by her elbow. She turned to me, and I acted completely out of character, using the child while doing so. "Thank you, Ruth, for coming along and helping your mother. It was a kind thing to do." Then I hugged her. I didn't even want to hug my own blood then, but that was the only way I could see to get closer to Margit.

"Oh," Ruth said, desperately embracing me back. Over her head stood Margit, visually touched by my display of gratitude, smiling almost enough to show teeth.

"And, Margit," I said, removing myself from the small girl and working my way to Margit. "Thank you. Really, for everything."

I embraced her and she hugged back. I could feel her breath on me, as well as the contours of her hips against mine, the strength of her arms around me, the softness of her breasts. I didn't want to let go. Her hair was silky against my arm, just as I imagined it would be. Her skin soft as the prairie sun would allow. She gave an extra squeeze before letting go.

"We'll see you tomorrow," she said. Ruth was already outside, heading toward their huge International truck. Margit smiled at me one last time, and then she was out the door, right behind her daughter.

After they left, I went into Janus's room. He lay as if he were asleep, with a dime-store novel across his chest, but the boy was wide-awake. I sat on the edge of his bed and tried to think of something to say. Only the other day I was worried about not having anything to speak to him about, and now, when there was so much to talk about—so much that had happened since that day—I still couldn't think of what to say. Soon, Janus spoke up, so I didn't have to think of what to say. "They seem like nice people," he said.

"I agree. Did I tell you I met them at the church?"

He nodded. "I think I've seen the girl at school. She's quiet."

"Yeah," I said. "Nice." I put my hand on his unharmed leg and rubbed it lightly. "I'm quiet, too."

"I know. We're all quiet here. Even Daddy was quiet."

"He was." Thinking of Daddy hushed me more. Janus and I sat there thinking about the silence of our family and listened to the wind outside. I said aloud, but almost in a whisper, "He's been dead four hundred and thirty-seven days. That is one hundred and twenty-two days after Trunk had to die."

"You've been keeping count of the days Daddy's been gone?"

"I don't want to. Each day, I wake up, I say, 'It's been another day.' Then I say the number of days it has been aloud. I don't mean to, but it's my prayer." It was more of a mantra, but I didn't know that then. "I don't remember my dreams. I try not to think about him when I wake up, but I tick off the days he's been gone each day, as if I'm counting up to something instead of . . . I don't know. It is as if in a certain amount of days, something is going to happen. When I hurt your leg—and, Janus, I'm so sorry about that—I thought I would wake up the next day and start counting over again. Maybe I'd say, 'It's been one day,' instead. That's what I thought. But no. It didn't change."

"Don't apologize again," he said. He then grew so still that if I didn't know better, I would have believed that he was sleeping.

I couldn't believe how much I said to him. It was the most I had spoken in a long time, if not forever, and I said it all in a whisper. The rant was a kind of confession, and I couldn't look at him. Again, I wanted the ritual of the Catholics. I wanted to be told something to do to make everything better.

"Might be you're waiting for something else to happen," Janus said. "You believe in God, right?"

"I don't know. I don't think so."

"Well, if you did, it might make sense; you could, or we could, be predestined for something."

"Just because I don't believe in God doesn't mean I don't believe in destiny."

The conversation seemed too smart for us. Almost too revealing. I stood up without looking at him.

"Hope you'll be walking soon."

"But you made us pray the other day. Did you go to church just to find the Svobodas?"

"Let's not talk about this, okay? Are you fine for now? Want me to read to you? I read similar books when I was your age. They opened up the world outside of Kansas."

"I don't know if I believe in God, either."

"Janus."

"Are we going to die? Nothing's growing. Mama's crazy. We don't seem too far behind Daddy and Trunk."

What was he expecting me to say? I could feel his eyes on me, waiting, but I didn't look at him. I said nothing. I just left the room.

Mama was at the kitchen table, chewing tobacco and rocking back and forth. "Didn't like those people here," she said. It was still disconcerting to see her up and about and even talking sometimes. I couldn't figure how to respond.

"They're helping out, Mama."

"Don't seem right. We can take care of our own." She spat a wad of tobacco on the floor, stood up, then left me alone in the kitchen. I felt like screaming. I wanted to hurt something. It was an almost beautiful day for me, and Janus ruined it with his talk of God and death, Mama with her insanity. I grabbed a rag and wiped the brown goo up off the floor. Where did she get tobacco from? Had it been chewed many times before and saved? I stood up too quickly and stars buzzed in my head, my eyes. Felt just like screaming.

I watched Margit from a nook near the garden tool shed. She pumped water as if she were doing it for herself, carefree and absentmindedly. When she had two full pails, she headed back toward the house. I followed at quite a few feet from behind her, being as silent as I could. When she went in, I waited awhile before getting near. I could hear her talking to Ruth, giving directions. I could tell that they were in the kitchen, so I walked toward that side of the house. I stood under the window and listened.

Margit was instructing Ruth to wash the dishes. I heard her pour water into the sink.

Next, I heard Margit walking away from the kitchen. I followed her footsteps. The walls were between us, she was inside, and I was outside. "Hello," I heard her say. I stopped. I was right beneath Janus's window. I tipped up on my toes and tried to get a look through the window, but it was too high up.

"Hello," Janus said. I could hear his bedclothes rustling as he moved around, probably trying to sit up to appear like a gentleman.

"You know what I have here? I have a bucket and a half of water," she said to Janus. He didn't respond, but I could hear him straightening himself out on the bed. "In my pocket," Margit continued, "I have a bar of soap and a washcloth. This is all for you."

"I have to take a bath?" Janus's voice was at its littlest. I looked away from the house and glanced around the yard. A bucket that I put out yesterday, the mouth down in order to dry out, rested near a tree. I quickly went for the bucket, then returned to beneath Janus's window. I situated the bucket, again mouth down, where the ground was almost flat. I stood atop it so I could see through the window. My nose was now just above the lower windowsill. I peeked in. From where I stood, I could see the back of Janus's head. He was alone, and he looked alone. He turned slightly, and I saw a sliver of his face. This is how Janus looked when he believed no one was watching. I felt so shameful that I almost quit the bucket and left for something to do, but Margit came back with a large bath towel.

"And here we are!" she said, holding the towel up to Janus as if it were an ermine coat he was buying.

"That's fine," he said. His voice sounded tiny. He was frightened and shy. I wanted to assure him that this was a good thing, that he'd appreciate it later, but I wasn't supposed to be there, so I remained hidden.

I could see Margit entirely—her hair, her face, her body—as she moved about the bedroom. She kept her dress and apron on, but the sleeves were rolled up past her elbows. I could see the shape of her muscles beneath her skin as she dunked the washcloth into one of the buckets and wrung it out. I could see how the butterscotch color of her forearms seeped into the usually hidden peach of her biceps and shoulders. I couldn't see from there the sun spots that had to have dotted her skin, but knowing they were there was enough.

"There is already a skin of dust atop the water," she said. "It's so hard to keep clean here."

"Do you have a husband?" Janus asked.

"Yes, I do. Mr. Svoboda runs the farm."

"You call him Mr. Svoboda?"

"I call him Peter. You call him mister. I also have four other children. One is just a baby." She walked to my brother and sat on the edge of his bed. "While I'm here, the boys take turns looking after the baby." She wiped Janus's face with the cloth, and then she dunked it back into the pail. She took the towel out again and wrung it. "Take off your shirt."

Janus took his shirt up slowly, exposing his thin frame and his sharp ribs to Margit. As he did this, she dipped the soap bar into the other pail and worked up a thick lather in her hands. She then spread the soap in quick, rough circles over Janus's skin. She talked as she worked to calm Janus down. His voice, first shaky, soon smoothed out, and as they talked with each other, I could tell that he was becoming more comfortable. He warmed up to her, and she treated him like her own child.

Mostly, I watched Margit. I got warm and desperate watching her. It was wrong to spy, but I couldn't stop following the trail of veins in her arms as she squeezed the towel. When stray hairs from her bun landed on her forehead, she'd wipe them away with the back of her hand, and I followed that movement, too. But something caught my eye from without the room, a quick but quiet motion just outside the door to Janus's room. I focused on that area—squinted my eyes nearly shut so that I may see better—and I saw Ruth. She stood there doing nothing. Every so often, she'd rock slowly in place, but mostly she only stood. She was watching, too, but what or whom I couldn't tell. Was it Janus? Did she look at his chest, which was bared willingly for Margit? Or was it Margit, the girl's mother? Was she feeling jealous?

Could she see me?

I shivered. And it was only then that I realized there was something more to Ruth than what I thought before. I wanted to warn them, Margit and Janus, of what Ruth was doing, but what could I say? I saw Ruth watch you like I watched you? I worked my way down off the bucket. I walked around the house toward the back door, and as I did so I tried to change my shamefaced expression to one of ignorant innocence. I was loud when I entered, hoping to scare Ruth away from outside my brother's bedroom. I let the door slam behind me and didn't remove my boots to cross the linoleum floor of the kitchen. My plan worked: Ruth soon walked quickly into the kitchen, her face still full of shame and something else I couldn't read.

When the Svobodas were over helping, Mama moved about the house, sighing, grunting, stating useless rules like "no one touches the silver" (which she sold almost a year ago), making as if she were working, making too much noise when she cooked, just making a nuisance of herself. Margit took it in stride. Ruth made herself smaller around my mother. I couldn't see how she was Margit's daughter.

Regardless of how I felt about Ruth, she obeyed her mother and worked well under Margit's orders. The two got things done. They cleaned the house thoroughly, helped with my mother, and cooked some meals. They also helped wash Janus, and Margit took him from his bed sometimes, gingerly walked him around as the doctor showed us.

Under Margit's care—or maybe it was the body's natural healing pattern from the injury—Janus's leg improved. The bruises were vanishing. He was also able to put a little pressure on his foot now and take one step with both feet on the floor.

I was truly thankful for having Margit over, for the company and the work. Having the Svobodas around allowed me to work the fields and to start building a lean-to. At that time, when we still had a little to barter with, I thought I should maybe find a few chickens, or maybe a couple of geese, to help sustain us. And out of obligation to the church that put me in touch with the Svobodas, I attended service each week. Margit would come at seven on Sunday to pick me up, and we'd drive into town. We'd sit in the same pew, she on one side, the kids lined up beside her, then me on the other side.

Less than two weeks of the Svobodas' visits, Ruth stopped coming. Margit said that she could handle things on her own. It was somewhat quieter without Ruth, and Mama didn't react as much with the strange girl gone, but she was still offended by Margit's presence. By then, Janus was able to make it from his bed to the window using a crutch. The weather was good, too, with a little bit of rain even (too little to mean something, of course). The house began to feel as if a stable family lived within its walls instead of the three us. Of course, we were missing Daddy, but we were getting along okay for the first time since his funeral.

Once when I was working outside, I saw Margit eating a sandwich. She was beneath the lean-to I had built for the future fowl. She saw me watching her and waved me over. I walked to her and stood at the chicken wire fence and called hello to her. "Have you eaten?" she called back. "I have another sandwich."

"No thank you, ma'am. I ate an early lunch."

"Come sit next to me. Keep me company."

I climbed over the chicken wire fence and joined her. She was chewing her food, and I had nothing to say. The cicadas buzzed around us where we couldn't see them, making the noise that I've always associated with hot days and summer. That sound makes one meditative. So the two of us were quiet before Margit spoke.

"How you all making it out here?" she asked.

I looked at her. Didn't she know? She was here every day. I watched her while she looked at her sandwich, a look of hunger but disappointment. She took another bite.

"We do okay," I said. "Considering. Getting tired of white biscuits and flour-and-water gravy, though."

"You all have enough meat?"

"About two times a week. But I hear it's going to get a lot harder to be got, meat. What about you all?"

"About the same. Ain't no meat on this sandwich." She took another bite. "Kills me to see my kids so scrawny," she said when her mouth was empty. "Ruth could barely lift an arm when she was out here with me. I wouldn't have had her out here if I didn't need her help to start. But what else was she going to do? It made her feel useful. And you have seen the others. My oldest son, Paul, going on fourteen, don't weigh more than eighty pounds. It ain't healthy."

"Thinking about getting some hens," I said. "Least that way, get some more protein in Janus through the eggs."

"Have you been picking up dried beans at the relief line?"

"Naw. Hadn't thought to. You know I hate asking for help."

"We all do." She put the last piece of sandwich into her mouth. I watched her from the corner of my eye. Her dimples faded in and out with each chew. "Thought about going out west?" she asked.

I didn't answer right away. I hadn't, but now that she'd said it, I wondered. "They say there's work out there. Good farmwork."

"Ah, I don't believe it." She made as if to spit, but thought better. "If that were the case, we'd all be out there. They'd send back for us."

"Harvesting berries, grapes, fruit from trees and stuff," I said. "Ain't the weather better out that way, too?"

"Hundreds, if not thousands of us wandering off west to get nothing but pennies on the dollar. Treat our men and kids like shit."

I gasped at her language.

"I said it," she went on. "And I hear tell of women being had like the cheapest kind of whores. Men and boys getting shot at for sleeping on private property. Killed, even. It's a load of bull."

"Then why do so many of us go?"

She looked at me squarely, her face angry, but her eyes had something else in them. "Out there, it's more of the same. Folks think they ain't got no choice, so they pack up and go like fools chasing rainbows. Bank takes their farm because they can't grow nothing to sell. They can't stay. Ain't no city work."

"I suppose I still have a choice. Daddy was always frugal. Didn't take any mortgage out on the homestead. And we have so little land that we never needed the extra money. Not until after he was gone. Come to find out a lot of what we thought we had, he used to save this place. If there was a market, I'd sell it."

"Yes," Margit said. Then she sat there, one knee up beneath her skirts, her face resting upon it, facing me. Her face was calming down as the anger left her, but she still had that odd look in her eyes. "Well, I best get back to work."

I stood up before her and then helped her to stand up. "I don't know how we'll ever repay you," I said. I held her elbow to help her get steady.

"God'll find a way. We talked about that. Plus, what else would I do with my time?"

"There's your family," I said.

"And there's Ruth. She can take care of things around there." Then she walked back to our house, leaving me to think back on what she had just said about Ruth, about her not being able, really, to lift an arm.

It was so dry that my lips hurt from chapping and my hands bled in the webs of the fingers. Dust settled there in my hands and I let it. It hurt at first, but it helped heal the cuts. I was out in the field picking up rocks by hand. Small boulders. I moved them from one barren area to another. The ground was so parched that it felt as if the field were paved over. I knew it could produce plants—not long ago, I had wandered through the rows of bright wheat. In the warm sun of those plentiful days, it smelled like bread baking. The soft, fertile ground was fine to roam shoeless. My toes would sink into some parts of the soil if I stood still. I used to love the feel of the cool almost-mud beneath my feet. I'd squish my toes to dig in, and Mama would yell at me for coming home with filthy feet.

I remember, too, before we got a real floor. The plank floors came in the mid-1920s. Before that, the floors were all dirt. We'd sweep them into a flat, neat plane in the morning when we woke, and again before going to bed at night. But even then, Mama would bother me about my dirty feet.

Those were the days when I went hunting for geese with Daddy and Trunk, when it rained regularly and what we planted grew, and when there was meat to eat. Thinking of them and those fat birds flying in from Canada, I looked up expecting to hear their honks, even though it was the wrong season. I expected, too, to see clouds puffed up and sharply white against the country blue sky, but what I saw was a pale blue tinted by dust that the wind lifted and moved around. Here, I was so deep in my reverie that I didn't hear Margit come up behind me to tell me that she was leaving for the day. I jumped a little.

"I should have called your name to let you know that I was coming," she said. "It's easy to get lost in your own self out here."

She was beautiful. I looked at her: her hair, the laugh lines, the freckles, the shape of her eyebrows, and the sheen of her skin. The mica in the dirt made her shimmer. *Beautiful* seemed like too little of a word, too common, but that was the only word I could think of. "Leaving for the day?" I said.

She nodded. "What is it, Greta?"

I grinned at her. "What?"

"You're looking at me like, well, I don't know. Like that."

I felt as if I'd been running. My breathing came quicker. "It may be the heat. I may need a drink."

She stood staring at me. She seemed concerned. "If that's it, we better get you some water." She turned, but I grabbed her. I grabbed her hand and held it. She turned back to me, and she looked very worried now. "What is it, Greta?"

"I'm not ready for you to leave just yet."

"Is there something else you need around the house?"

I shook my head. "It's a calm day."

She turned fully to me and faced me. She held my hand back and we looked at each other, studied each other, as a woman who is about to leave her house studies her reflection in the mirror. We stood this way for a minute or two, her hand in mine and our hands sweating together, before the wind picked up a little, bringing dust devils and the flyaways from our buns with it.

"You think it's going to be a storm?"

"We should probably go. You should probably get back." I let go of her hand, but then she grabbed for mine. We returned to the farmhouse that way—hand in hand.

After our first impromptu lunch, Margit and I made a regular date of meatless sandwiches under the lean-to. With her, I spoke more than I spoke with anyone else.

To her, I told my hopes and dreams, and with me, she shared her dreams. Soon, I understood the look she got when she talked about going out west and about the economy. It was fear, and when she was afraid, I got scared, too.

One day, she was quiet through most of the meal, and when she spoke, it was about that potential move. "Peter doesn't think we can make it here much longer," she said with her sandwich only half eaten in her hands. "We were one of those families that took money out when times were good. Who knew fat days like that would end? We were growing wheat without trying, growing alfalfa and corn, too. We ran out of storage room for the grain and had to rent silo space. And we bought everything money could buy then. Ruth got dresses out of the Sears, Roebuck catalog. We bought a toy train set and even a pedal car for the boys. I felt unholy with how well we were doing, and greedy for buying Ruth's dresses instead of making them, for buying those useless things for the boys. But we had the money. We had the means." She stopped talking. She cried without sobbing. "I thought Peter wanted to hold on to that land. Hasn't it been in his family for over fifty years? He's just going to walk away? I was sure he'd be the last person to leave."

Unlike my family and Margit's, Peter's family came when the land was still being wrestled from the Comanche people. Peter's people were among the first to break through the buffalo grass and plant grass.

"No," Margit said. "He was trying hard to keep it, but the bills kept coming while the price of wheat kept falling. You know how it is. It won't rain and it won't rain. I can't even read the clouds anymore. The sky looks just like a soaker, and then nothing comes but dirt."

"You want to go, too." My chest heaved in and out, and I breathed a little heavier.

"I don't know. Peter used to talk about it all the time. Now, he says he has other ideas. He does say leaving Kansas is still a possibility."

"What other ideas? What does he mean by that?" My heart beat faster in my chest, but my breathing slowed considerably. Margit only shook her head. She looked so frightened, I wanted to hold her and offer my protection. Of course, I didn't want Peter to do anything rash, but I didn't want them to go away from me. I didn't want Margit and my lunches together to stop. I asked, "What do you want to do?"

"Oh, Greta, I don't know. Who can know? We're all so hungry, so tired. I don't think my youngest is going to make it." She breathed a frightened, choked sob that rang loud against the wall of the prairie sky. Then she let go. Instinctively, I grabbed hold of her and held her close. And we stayed that way as she cried.

Margit invited me to Sunday dinner. I refused, thinking of what she told me about how much they were hurting, but she insisted. The table spread wasn't impressive, but I wasn't expecting much, and I tried to eat as little as possible.

The two oldest boys got the most food. One, Paul, talked like crazy about everything. He wanted to try his luck in California. He talked about if not fruit, then oil; if not oil, then gold. "And maybe I'll keep going, across the ocean," he said. The other boy, Ezekiel, was quiet. He only spoke when spoken to. I recognized him as the kid who had stopped me from clubbing Janus, but neither one of us mentioned it, and I appreciated his silence. Peter got a good amount of food, too, but he didn't eat much. He passed food to Ruth's plate or one of the older boys when Margit wasn't looking. He looked almost dead, Peter did, and I thought about all the things Margit shared with me, especially that he had said he had other ideas besides going west.

The baby was quiet, even for a baby. He was mostly in his crib and barely made a noise. In fact, I was there for almost two whole hours, and I didn't hear him cry once. I peeked at him before I left. He looked nearly dead, too. "Hi, baby," I said. I smiled my admiration for his family to see, but I was already mourning him. I didn't want to touch him.

The dinner was dismal in spite of my and the Svobodas' effort. I was happy when Margit offered to take me back home. We drove for a bit, then parked on the side of the road. We held hands like young girls and sat close to each other. The heat from her skin and the now setting sun made me lean toward the passenger window. To be comfortable, she leaned into me, on my shoulder.

"How old are you, Greta?" Margit asked me.

"I'll be twenty come December."

"Is that it?"

"Do I look older? Or younger?"

"Why haven't you married, Greta?"

I shrugged. There were two reasons, and I sat there thinking how to tell them to Margit.

"Have you ever been with a man?"

It was a question from Providence. I nodded.

"May I ask who? Did you love him?"

I nodded again.

"Do you mean that I may ask, or that you loved him?"

I took a breath before answering. I told her all about the night with my father, leaving out messy details and keeping in my fear and anger. I told her how I knew that it was something wrong, but that on a level it was enjoyable. "It was just one time," I told her.

"Greta, I'm so sorry. That's horrible."

"It's really—" I stopped. "I did love him, though. I do love him."

"But not like that."

"No, not like that. But it was only that once. He never did anything like that again."

"I think you're comparing men to your father. No one is ever going to measure up."

"Probably not." We spoke slowly as if we had all the time in the world and no one else depended on us to return to our homes.

I had told her only one of the reasons.

"That is a bad experience, Greta. It is abominable. I believe you can fall in love with someone if you gave it a try. You won't know that until you let another man touch you. You don't know what it's like to love a man you could consider your equal. Someone who is near you in thinking and goals, who you can have children with. It's nothing to be ashamed of, but something to thank God for."

"You're probably right."

"You look like you'd make good children."

"Who'd want children when there's nothing to eat?"

Margit sighed. I thought about that listless baby back at her house. She came in closer and rested on my shoulder more. I let go of her hand and put my arm around her shoulders. Then I stroked her hair. I let my fingers get caught in the natural ringlets that were piled on her head, and I slowly worked them out of the curls. "Janus can just about walk now," I said.

"He's a good boy," Margit said. "Smart, too." She seemed downright sleepy. I was afraid that she'd end the day so that she could get back home and to her bed. I shook one of my legs anxiously.

"He is. I feel really bad about it," I said.

"He knows that."

I continued to stroke her hair. Then I kissed her forehead. She didn't move away. I wasn't expecting to kiss her, but I did it. I kissed her again. She sat up a little and looked at me. "We'll still be friends, won't we? When he heals completely?"

"Maybe this is God at work," I said. Then I kissed her mouth. She closed her eyes and kissed back.

"It's been so long since Peter's done anything to me," she said. And it was okay. It was perfectly okay. The still day, the late sun shining down on her International truck. The cicadas buzzing. Our bellies slightly full from the food she got from relief and cooked up with Ruth. I had talked to them while they worked in their warm kitchen. We three had laughed together. And it was natural now, us kissing and loving each other in the cab of her truck.

We hunched down on the bench seat so that no one could see, our kisses desperate and sloppy. We missed each other's lips, kissing the edges of each other's mouths, chins, and noses. We groped clumsily at each other's bodies, feeling the differences and similarities of our breasts, hips, and thighs. When we made mistakes, we laughed, at first nervously, then comfortably, but it wasn't long until we got into a rhythm. Then we were lying side by side and facing each other, nearly falling off the bench seat. We were so close together that I could feel her body rise and fall with her breathing. I could feel her skin pucker as I exposed it to the air by taking her clothes off.

We were sweating, mewing, groaning like farm cats in heat. Everything was so slick with perspiration on her and me that I should not have been surprised to find her wet between her thighs, but still it caught me off guard. I got goose bumps with the feel of her. My spine tingled as if a cool breeze blew across it. I got greedy for the taste of the salt on her skin. I let my lips and, sometimes, my tongue touch her bare skin. I let my hands massage her, move her flesh; let my fingers prod her as if hers was my own body, as if I were out in the tall buffalo grasses before they were mown down to nothing, before the sun burned everything to tufts of waste that blew away with everything else—as if it were those days when it was quiet like now, and I could hear anyone coming, and I could pull up my drawers, lower my dress, and wipe my fingers on the grass around me. With Greta, I lifted her skirt, I pulled down her underwear, I rubbed her hair there, slightly red, fuzzy, and womanly. I traced the opening to her vagina, and I felt her push back, then pull me in. I followed the movements of her hips that guided me inside of her, and I felt with my fingertips the differences of her muscles from mine. I felt her hesitate again, but briefly, then she moved with me.

When it was over, we held each other. One of us elbowed the gear shift into neutral, and we began to roll slowly forward on the rough shoulder of the dirt road. Margit saved the car from going much farther. The truck stopped, and then we scrambled up, dressing as we did so. When we were on the road toward my home, and dressed, we were still breathing heavily.

I got chicks. I bought six from a neighbor up the road who had just joined the caravan going west. Janus was really broken up about their leaving, because then he and Ezekiel would be two of only a few boys around the same age in our community. So many of us were going now, or had gone, that it was almost a ghost town. The Catholic and the Baptist churches closed, boarded up their stained-glass windows that were at ground level. Those of us who were left first stood guard over our missing neighbors' vacated homes and the belongings they couldn't carry, but after some time, when things started getting really serious, we'd take to searching the abandoned houses for provisions. Sometimes we had to break locks, but mostly the doors were left open. We would go into those mostly empty rooms, filled with only the biggest furniture—the pieces that could not be carried atop a farm truck—that sat covered with thick dirt. The dirt came from the dust storms, which were growing more numerous and worse. Spiders and insects had taken over every corner of the rooms, the windowsills, the cabinets, when they could. Sometimes, when spider eggs hatched and you were there for it, you could hear the baby spiders crawling over the surfaces. Their patter sounded like a soft rain on dry ground. Still, even with the infestations of the deserted homes, there was always something to be salvaged.

We sometimes found dusty jars of preserves or pickles and boxes of grain that still held edible food that was left behind and not yet eaten by the mealworms and summer moths. We greedily ate all the food we found, working our way around all the gritty dirt that would get in the boxes or the pots in which we cooked our food. Sometimes we ate the food where we found it, standing and using our hands as utensils, or sitting carefully in the cloth-covered chairs.

I fed the chicks some of the old grains we gleaned, and they found their own food in the dirt. Margit told me to keep them in the kitchen garden, so that they may eat the bugs that bother the plants there. Not much was coming up in the garden because of the heat, dust storms, and grasshoppers (there were too many for my birds to eat), but I had a few scraggily vegetables the chicks could pick around. After they were in the garden for a few days pecking at the dirt, some of the leaves on the plants were less full of holes and looked healthier. Janus, who was now able to go outside—but walked with a considerable limp—came and played with the birds as they grew. Eventually, they were his chicks. And soon, they were his chickens.

Margit and I still shared our moments in her truck, under secluded trees, under the lean-to, and, once, in my bed. It was odd and awkward at first, but we grew used to being together. We couldn't get enough of each other for a while. I loved to look at her when she was naked, after we were together bringing each other up and up again. Her skin, covered in sweat and mica-filled dust, sparkled like glitter in the sun. Her stomach was soft from bearing all those kids, and I'd run my hands over it. Her breasts were full, her nipples a burnt brown color. I loved the smell of her, of whatever she used to wash with and how it worked in the sun.

I was happy. Janus knew it and told me one day that he appreciated having Margit around to cheer our lives. "I'm glad she still comes around even though I'm much better."

I smiled at him. "I am, too. She is very special, isn't she?"

Also, Janus and I had things to talk about. Our meals were no longer silent and uncomfortable. Really, Margit Svoboda changed the mood of our little farm. I think Mama noticed it, too. She stopped complaining so whenever Margit was around, and she started taking some meals with Janus and me.

It wasn't perfect. Almost each time we met, Margit would worry that we were being sinful. "I do with you what I should be doing with Peter," she'd say. "I know he's not interested, but this is being unfaithful."

"It's not really," I'd say. It was always my argument. "I'm not a man, so it's not really cheating. What we're doing is a lot different."

"I don't see how. It brings us to the same point. And we can't conceive this way, so it seems like an affront to God. It's not natural for two women to be together this way."

"It seems like, but it's not. I'm sure God is pleased we can still find beauty in the world, in spite of the storms and things not growing. In spite of the money not coming in. Margit, isn't it wonderful that we have each other?"

We'd go back and forth on the wrongs and rights of what we were doing until I made her feel good again, and she'd forget about the sin of it all until we met again. I started to see it as a game we played, so her complaints never got to me.

Sometimes, too, she would talk about her youngest child. She'd never say his name. She'd only call him "the baby" or, sometimes, "baby": "Baby isn't eating well," and "Baby keeps coughing." But she didn't mention him or much of her family that often.

Janus and I went on one of our shopping trips to the houses of neighbors who'd headed west. We broke into the Schöpps' home. When times were good, they were a rich family. They bought clothes from Sears and from the shop in Dodge City, over a day's trip for them. They had come back with clothes like nothing anybody in Kismet had ever seen. Difficult stitches made possible by only the finest machines or the most-skilled hands. Sleeves that fell off the shoulders and complemented the arm. Perfect pleats and falling waistlines. Feather boas. And for the men, pin-striped suits and spats. Silk ties and satin shirts. Cuff links of bone or mother-of-pearl and trilby hats. Of course, they couldn't take it all with them, so Janus and I put them on, outfit by outfit. We strutted around the Schöpps' house, the suits too large for Janus and the dresses too tight for me. We made trails in the dust with the hemlines and noise in those rooms that were quieted by the Schöpps' absence. "This had to be a kind of beautiful place when times were good," Janus said. "Did you ever come here then?"

"I think I was invited once or twice. You know, Theresa was my age. It's not that we were in the same circles, or that I was in any circle. I think there was a party or two here, from what I remember." We dusted the sofa off the best we could, beat the cushions, and then sat down. The dirt from our dusting floated thickly in the air as we sat and talked.

Janus, always the honest one, said, "I didn't know you attended any parties."

"There was school." I took his hand and held it as we sat and talked. He and I showed affection in this way, and it was all Margit's doing, I know. I said to Janus, "In school, I tried things."

"And now?"

"Now? I have on this lovely flapper dress." I lifted the hem from where I sat, stretching the pleats out. "What about you? You're not quite at that age yet, right? The age of parties."

"Parties kind of died out along with everything else. You know, I have friends a little. And like I said, I've seen Ruth Svoboda around, but she's a little strange."

"You shouldn't talk about people like that."

"She is, though. She moves like she's in mud. She talks slow. She's constantly in her hair."

"She's fine. She helped us a lot, along with Margit."

"I saw you and Margit."

My breath caught. "What?"

"I saw you and Margit. Out by the tractor."

"How? I mean, yeah? Of course you saw us. We're always together."

"I know. I was going over to show you how well I walked, and I saw you two. I didn't want to interrupt. What was going on?"

"Did you tell anyone?"

"Who would I tell? What would I tell? You two were holding each other and . . . I don't know what. Never mind."

"And what?"

"Were you kissing her? Like men and women kiss?"

"Please don't tell Mama."

"You know I don't talk to her."

My heart was beating too hard and the breaths I took were too big. I inhaled the dirt from the couch, the other furniture, the house, the yards, the fields, the plains. "Let's get our regular clothes on. Let's just get our regular clothes, Janus. Let's leave." I let go of his hand. I noticed my own was sweating.

"But what does that mean? You and Mrs. Svoboda together like that? Does this have anything to do with you never marrying?"

"Get those fancy clothes off, Janus." I stood and got myself ready, then grabbed the food and other things I had planned to bring with me. "I have to get out of here. I can't breathe."

I was coughing as I gathered the things. I could see the dust and dirt floating through the slatted windows. I thought dumbly as I made my way out that the sun was never clear inside anymore. I left the Schöpps' house and walked, dropping things as I went. I did not stop to pick them up. I could hear Janus calling my name, telling me to wait. I could hear him stop and pick up the things I dropped. I could hear the blood running from one ear to the other ear, feel blood running to my nose and to the base of my neck.

During the Dust Bowl years, there were a lot of days that looked promising. We would get stretches of days with nothing but sun and blue skies. I had begun to hate the color blue. I would wake up in the morning before the sun rose to get the day going on the farm, and each day I'd hope for an overcast sky full of clouds thick with rainwater. When the sun would come up, yellow and round in a clear blue sky after I'd gotten my hopes up for a rainy day, I was sick with frustration. But there were some days when a cloud would appear, or two clouds. I'd spend all day looking up at the sky, following the path of that lone cloud and wondering if it would break open and rain. I couldn't tell if those days were better or worse than the clear ones. On those days with a cloud or two, I would shake with anticipation. My teeth and gums were like I sucked copper all day. I kept spitting in the dry fields, trying to get that metallic taste out of my mouth.

In 1931, the wheat was high on our farm, yellow as happiness, amber waves as in the song. It was tall on everyone's farm. The money was only waiting to come in with the harvest. Then it stopped raining.

Those first few weeks with Margit were just like that. It seemed as if the weather would always come through for us and always go as it was supposed to. It seemed, too, that Margit and I would sow love forever, but then her baby died. He wasn't getting enough nutrition, and he just would not thrive. The constant dust could not have helped matters, either. Margit said that he had coughed like an old smoking, drinking man the days before he died.

When Mama, Janus, and I went to the small funeral and saw that baby laid out in the little pine box, we all remarked how strong the Svobodas looked, leaning on one another. Margit did cry—they all did—but even so, they kept a certain decorum about them. And Margit, even with her pain, was elegant in her mourning. Her blond curls were cleaned and scented. She patted a gloved hand over her locks often to check for dust buildup. I could see the dingy palms of the white satin gloves: they, like everything else, were covered with dirt.

I could not help but feel a pang of jealousy when I watched Peter comfort Margit. I wanted to be able to touch her as he did. I wanted to lightly run my hand through her hair and caress her neck. I tried to catch her eye, but she wouldn't look toward me more than a second. What I saw between her and her husband was clear to me. Theirs was a love of family, a love of duty, solidarity in creating a life and losing it. I knew that Peter was hurting just as much as Margit, and I knew that their lives were forever changed.

I cried at the funeral. Quick, polite tears. Partly for the baby whose name was never used, partly for the inevitable end of my relationship with Margit.

Margit came to help after her baby died, but we saw her less and less. And when we talked, very often the subject of her children would come up. Before she would leave for home each time, she would end up talking about her dead baby, and she would leave with tears in her eyes. I was hurting for her loss, but I was also hurt that I got to see so little of her alone. When she came, she preferred to talk with my whole family instead of being with just me.

Then Peter killed himself. He got himself pulled into the power takeoff of his tractor. He was mangled up into pulp and chipped bone. Their son Ezekiel found him out in the field, bit by bit. He wasn't sure what he was finding until he got right up on his father. The tractor was almost dead because the gas was running low, but it was going. I couldn't imagine what seeing that had done to the boy, but when I slept, I could see a young, tanned arm reaching out, as if it were mine, picking up chunks of denim and skin, bloody and chewed to jagged shapes. As I dreamed on, the pieces of Peter would get bigger, with thick flesh filling out the skin pieces. It would smell like slaughter day when times were still good, when my own father was still alive and we had pigs and even a few cows. And when I saw the face, it was always Daddy's, not Peter's. Those dreams made me wake up quickly, jumpy with the smell of copper and iron in my nose. The smell of blood.

I always wondered how Ezekiel would grow up. Often after that, I'd send Janus to go to try to talk to him, to do what boys do, but Janus said that Ezekiel was quieter than us. He said Ezekiel was reluctant to leave anyone alone in his family. "He wanders the perimeter of their farm. I think he's protecting them from something that he can't see," Janus said. I thought that maybe Ezekiel was looking for pieces of Peter he may have missed.

Peter's death was called an accident—the insurance company wanted to call it suicide but couldn't find the proof for its claim. We all knew better. We knew the insurance people were right, but no one would have told an agent that, though they sent an agent around asking after Peter. With his death, the Svobodas could stay in Seward County and keep their land. We knew he sacrificed himself for his family and their home. Though Paul, the oldest Svoboda son, would go west within a year, the rest would and could stay.

The rain had stopped coming again for me. I thought Peter's death would eventually draw us closer, but my affair with Margit ended.

Even though the hens had the lean-to, I took to spending time there to mope around in the dry dirt. The hens rooted around me, eating their feed and the little bugs that wriggled in the dust. The chickens strutted over me as if I was just part of the obstacle I created. I didn't shoo them away.

Janus would try to talk to me, to which I'd offer minimal response, but mostly I ignored him. Things were falling back to how life was prior to Janus's accident: quiet meals, quiet house, quietness. I pulled myself together enough to attend Peter's funeral, but nothing further than that. Janus said to me, "It's like Dad died all over again."

I was not down long. About a month later, I sat out in the tractor in the middle of the field. I didn't have anything to do with the tractor; I was just in it because it felt right. I was thinking that I knew two things: one was that Janus and Mama needed me, and the other was that I could not bring myself to die. I could only hope that I would die, that I would get some kind of sickness, or I'd get run over by the tractor accidentally, or anything. I just did not want to be alive anymore.

While I was there reveling in my funk, I felt something land on my thigh, and I jumped in fright and from the shock the touch generated. It was hot and dry in those days; being touched was sometimes electric. I looked down to see whose hand was on my thigh and saw that it was Margit, smiling up at me, the sun lighting up her hair like fire. She gave my thigh a few swift swats. I wanted to say that charge was from something else. She said something, but I couldn't hear over the wind, even though we were so close. "Margit!" I beamed. I was happy to see her and ready to forget her absence. I checked to see that the tractor's brake was on to be sure and jumped down right beside her.

"Let's have us a seat," she said. She smoothed out the back of her skirt and sat down with her back against one of the wheels of the tractor. I sat beside her, and then we both stared at each other, smiling. But it wasn't as I imagined. She was straightening out her skirts and smiling girlishly. I wasn't covering her with kisses. I wasn't overjoyed. I was just happy to see her.

"You shouldn't walk up on a lonely woman like that," I said, "by herself in a tractor. It's dangerous."

"But you weren't moving. The engine ain't even on."

"Doesn't have much gas."

She turned away from me and looked out on the fields. It was a while before she spoke again, but she didn't even have to speak. I knew what she would say before she said it. "You're not doing this again, are you?" she asked. "Hiding in plain sight?"

I was quick with my answer because I knew the question was coming. "I don't know. I've been kind of depressed with you gone."

"I miss you, too. But I came to tell you this: little Janus has been out to our farm to see us."

"He has, has he?"

"He's really worried about you."

I looked at my hands resting in my lap. "Guess I kind of wanted you to come back around."

She brought her hand up to my shoulder and rested it there. I, too, looked out on the fields and felt silly for sitting here in the dirt. There was nothing, no need for a tractor. Just dirt atop dirt all around, and even some of that had blown away in the dust storms, piled up in quick little hills.

I looked at Margit. She took her hand from my shoulder and ran it lightly down my cheek. "I don't think I have time for that now, Greta. With Peter gone, that whole farm's just my responsibility."

"I suppose so." I heard myself say it in a steady voice, no hint of tears or disappointment. I wanted to say that her children were strong enough to take some of that responsibility, that Ezekiel and Paul could all but run the little bit of land that was doing anything by themselves, but I kept quiet. "What am I doing out here, Margit?"

"I don't know. Janus needs you, though."

"He does. I know. I just want so much to be loved. You understand that, right?"

"You are loved. Your brother and your mother both love you dearly, Greta."

"I know, but I need something more."

"Are you talking about like what I had with Peter? Is that what you want?"

"You mean a man?"

"I mean a man."

I tried to picture myself being a wife. Not working outside but inside, cooking pies and rearing kids. I thought about having babies pull at my apron, dirty hands and sloppy kisses. There'd be dirty diapers and endless questions, noise, and botheration. I'm sure there were good things, too, but I didn't know what they were. "I don't think I want that, either. I guess I don't know what I want."

"You have a long time to figure it out, dear. You're relatively young and you're quite the looker. If you ever want a man, you'll have no trouble finding one."

"You think so? Oh, why am I getting excited for? I don't like men, Margit. I don't ever want one. I don't want a wife's life. I like it out here in the fields."

"Ain't shit out here in the fields."

"You got that right. Well, right now, but this can't last forever."

We sat there together, her hand resting again, this time in my lap. We gazed into each other's eyes as lovers would, but I didn't love her. Not like that. Margit was a good friend, but I was not really mourning the loss of her anymore, just fretting over my loneliness. I still liked her, though, and I liked the touch of her. I took her hand from my lap and drew it up to my lips, kissed it right in the center of the palm. A current from my dry lips ran through her dry hand. It felt like flipping a switch, turning on a bright lamp. I pulled her to me, my hands on her face, and then I kissed her, long and sensually. She kissed back.

We made love beside the tractor. In our excitement, our bodies generated enough sweat that we glided together painlessly. Easily, our hands found crevices and openings. We pulled off some of our clothes but left most of them on. Our hands caressed and massaged the familiar haunts of each other's bodies. Our lips and tongues found bare skin and kissed and licked liberally. Dust got into our hair, into the folds of our clothes and skin, but we ignored it. We partly hoped the tractor's great tires would hide us from anyone who happened to cross the field, but we didn't care.

Even as I made love to her, I knew it was the last time. When I felt myself getting too comfortable, I made it uncomfortable: I bit her bottom lip, her chin, her nipple hard enough to leave a mark. I let her knee me unknowingly in my side. Or maybe she knew. Maybe she wanted to hurt and to be hurt, too. I was not generous with my fingers this time, forcing most of my hand inside of her, and she was brutal, too. But after each jab, we soothed each other. We made it better.

It was the last time, but that was all right. I finished knowing that there would be other women. At least, I told myself that there may be others.

Margit and I lay in each other's arms and let the sun dry our skin. I stroked the soft flesh of Margit's inner thigh. The sky had threatening clouds stacking on top of each other, unusually dark, almost ethereal, but it did not feel like rain. It was only the start of the next dust storm.

"What will you do now, Margit?"

"Return home and continue being that bitter old widow."

"You're not bitter, nor are you old."

"When you're a widow, you have to be. At least the bitter part—taking on both roles as mother and father does something to you. Children's laughter ain't no longer cute. Especially when you're one child less than when you started. I have no right to be happy."

When the day started getting too dark to see each other's smiles, we dressed and walked back to my house, hand in hand. I kissed her goodbye in front of her truck and never saw Margit in that way again.

After that day, I tried to redefine myself out from under other people's shadows. I got more birds. When they'd sadly die in the dust storms, I would get birds again through trade or from the little money I could scrape up here or there. I built chicken coops, each new one more elaborate than the last one, to protect them from the dust. But these storms had no forecast, and like rainstorms, you never really knew when one was coming until it was right upon you. So the chickens would die. They'd be caught out in the storm, running around in the darkness. We could never see them because the dust made it too dark to see anything, but I would imagine them with their heads up to the sky, their mouths open to the falling dirt. It always hurt me to know it was happening, but I was powerless. I couldn't go out to save them without hurting myself.

When I convinced myself to become my own person, I thought that I had to change completely. First I started dressing like a man, which didn't work. I am old-fashioned and prefer a skirt to slacks any day. Then I thought I'd have to be very feminine, but that was too much for me. I tried lipstick for a short while and I hated it. I refused any other makeup. Too much femininity kept me away from the fields, and I needed to be there, even if the fields did not need me.

I hunted before, but I only did so much, to protect everyone's crops from jackrabbits. It was fun, too, to shoot the rodents in our yard. I wanted to hone my hunting skills, so was constantly at the library for books on hunting. I wanted to talk to hunters in our community, but everyone was going out west. Or everyone was so preoccupied with his failures that he didn't want to talk hunting at a time like this.

Another activity I tried was something historically considered women's work, and that was quilting. I joined a quilting group with other women in the community. We'd have bees where we could talk for hours. Mostly, I listened, but the other women considered me a friend. We'd exchange recipes, secrets, chores, and advice. From the women in that group, I learned how to make a flakier pie shell and how to make food from commodities that were not biscuits or fried chicken. Some of the women came and went—mostly because so many families left Kismet for work—but there was a core group that stayed loyal to the bees. I was part of it. And even after the drought and war were over, we quilted. Inviting new women in and saying goodbye to those who left the Plains. We buried some, attended weddings of others, and invited daughters and granddaughters into our group.

Some of the women were like me, and they were not hard to discover. We'd find ways to let ourselves be known. I would let my hand touch some other woman's who was sitting next to me, and if she did not move it away immediately, I'd look at her. If she looked back at me with anything resembling interest, I'd ask her for a quick walk to get some air. Then I would let things happen organically from there. In that way, I had many lovers until I got tired of the game.

But those relationships happened much later. I note them here because I want there to be something happy about all this, about my future. Because after Mama died, the dismal world Janus and I lived in only got worse.

In 1935, our mother got caught outside in a dust storm. It was the storm that would make it into history books, the storm that we named Black Sunday. Mama was out walking, looking for dandelion greens to cook up for us. I was outside hanging up clothes to dry. Janus was inside, reading one of the many books he picked up from the library. None of us expected anything, of course; the day was clear and still. In fact, it was one of the most beautiful days that spring. We were sure that we would not see a dust storm.

But then the temperature had dropped—plummeted in minutes—and the sky went from sunlight to darkness in seconds. On the northern horizon, I saw it coming, like evil incarnate: a gigantic, billowing ball of dirt. I looked up and up, and I couldn't see the sky from the darkness. I didn't know whether to go for the chicken coop or the clothes. In a second, I decided the clothes could be washed or remade, so I ran to the coop and shooed and shoved as many of the hens I could into the structure I'd built. I had chinked white clay between the slats of the coop to keep the dust out, but I knew that this storm would be too much. I shooed the rooster, who strutted around like he was Mr. Big Shot, into one of the older, smaller henhouses I had made. I was worried about our house, too; we had taken down the wet sheets and newspaper we used to keep the dust out because, really, we thought it would be the end of it. We thought the storms were over. I knew I wouldn't make it before the storm hit to replace all of that.

Next, I went back for the clothes, but as I ran toward the house, I stopped when a gust of wind hit me like an unmoving force. Our truck lost traction in front of me and skidded, seemingly all on its own, but with the help of the wind. The truck turned so that it was facing me, and I didn't know which way to run.

"Greta," my brother yelled over the din of the wind. He was on the porch, facing the dust cloud moving quickly toward us.

I held up a hand to him, telling him to wait a moment. The truck decided to go left. It moved sideways, but the tires stayed set and I could hear them scraping across the dirt. A horrendous noise. Later after the storm, we saw how two of the tires had buckled. When the truck was out of the way, I yelled to my brother. "Speak up," I said. "Yell louder." The storm muffled everything and talking in a normal voice was like talking to one's self.

"Mama is still out there," he said.

Oh, shit. I was not sure what to do. "Go back inside, Janus," I said.

He looked worriedly at me, anxious to do something. I knew the look; I'm sure that I had a similar expression on my face. I ran to him, gesturing for him to go back in the house. I was going to go and look for Mother, but I turned and saw that dust cloud coming toward me and that it was bigger than any storm I had seen before. What could I do but go in the house?

"What about Mother?" Janus asked.

"I don't know. I can't think of what to do."

"I'm really scared, Greta."

"Me, too."

We stood there in our kitchen talking to each other. I tried to brush some of the dirt off me.

"If I go out there for her, then we'd both be out there."

"And then?" he said.

I turned to look out the window and Janus joined me. We both searched through the yard from where we stood, looking for movement that wasn't wind or dust. Soon, we couldn't see nearly anything at all. It was quiet and loud at the same time: the roar of the wind and crackling of static electricity silenced everything. It was dark both inside and out. Shouting, I asked Janus if he knew where the rope was. He said he did and told me to grab his hand. I reached out, unable to see my hand, and he reached out, too. After what seemed to be forever, we touched hands, but jumped apart immediately, having been shocked strongly by the static generated from the storm. "Let's try again," I said. I licked my hand, picking up dirt on my tongue, and held it out for my brother. Eventually, he found it and grabbed it and we were moving, walking blindly toward the rope, Janus leading.

We were in the mudroom. I knew it by the way we stepped down into the room, moved left then right then straight ahead. I heard Janus knock tools off the shelves until he found the rope. We worked so that I tied an end around him and the other around me. We left the house tethered together. "Should I stay here," he asked, "or you?"

"You stay. I'll go look for her. Don't leave the porch."

"Here," he said, and he turned on a flashlight he held in his hand. Passed it to me. I pointed it ahead, and all I could see was dirt, both fine and gravel-sized, coming at me.

I left the house and walked as far as the rope would let me, stopping when I felt resistance from my little brother back on the porch, turning back only when the rope was taut. I closed my eyes against the storm, squinted as if I were facing the sun. I tried my best to keep my mouth closed, opening up at intervals to call out for Mama, only to get no response. For what seemed like hours, but could only have been minutes, I searched blindly. I didn't find her.

I followed the rope back to Janus and our house. Once inside with him, I tried to brush as much dust as I could off my face, my clothing. Janus didn't ask me anything. I didn't say a word. The flashlight's battery had died.

When I got cleaned up as best I could, we sat together. We had worked our way into the living room, where we sat to wait it out. Braving the risk of shock, I held him in my lap. And in this way, we waited for the storm to blow away.

We couldn't see a thing for quite some time. It was like night. No, it was darker than night. Particles from the storm rained onto the roof. Still, no real rain. I don't know how long it lasted, but when it was over, dust got into our noses and mouths even though we had handkerchiefs over our faces. Even though the doors and windows were closed, many pieces of furniture had a thick layer of dust. Mounds of dirt had drifted into the corners. Later, too, we would find that most of the chickens died almost instantly. Only two little ones survived, who were all but covered by the hens that huddled in the corner of the coop. On others' farms, we would hear about people losing the animals that survived the drought and dearth of grain to the dust. Finding cows and horses with all orifices filled, sometimes days later, and made like mummies because the dirt preserved them.

Janus and I ventured out as soon as we thought it was safe. It didn't take too long to find her; she was on the side of the road about a half mile away from the house. She was completely covered in dirt. Before we took her back to the house, before we even stood her up, we cleared her nostrils and mouth with our fingers. We scooped dust from the hollows of her eyes. The dirt lined her wrinkles, making her up like a comic book charac-ter—heavily outlined in black. We slapped at her face and blew into it, chattering about nothing at all, assuring her that she would be okay, trying to keep everything together. She wasn't talking. She hardly moved. And every time it appeared that we'd cleared enough dirt away from her mouth, she'd cough up mud and, eventually, blood.

When we figured we had cleaned her up enough for the trek, we carried her back to the house, with me doing most of the carrying, which I didn't mind, though she was a big woman. She was breathing, but it was difficult for her. We knew what would happen and we couldn't help our guilt, though there was really nothing we could have done. Tears and sweat streaked muddy pathways across Janus's face. I could only imagine how I looked.

"You'll be okay, Mama," he said.

"I don't—" she started, but she began coughing. The act shook her hard. We had to stop. She coughed until she spat, then spat until she threw up. When the spell was over, she wiped her mouth with her apron, which smeared a mess of mud, blood, and chewed-up biscuits and gravy all over her face. "I need to sit down," she said. "I need water."

Janus and I resumed our work, one on each side of her, half carrying our mother home. Between us, she shivered in the cold and in her sickness, and every so often, she'd cough. At home, we cleaned our mother the best we could, having to put her in the bathtub and remove all her clothes. She didn't resist. She slept through most of it. She only coughed—and now what came up was mostly blood. Janus said prayers over her and I said nothing, just waited for her to wake up fully and to swear at us. I wanted her to say that she'd be okay.

In that storm, our mother had lost the vision in her left eye, but that didn't matter too much. We learned later that she had dust pneumonia and that it was only a matter of days before she would die. The news saddened me, but I also felt a little freer.

Dead chickens aren't completely a loss. Janus and I had meat for a few weeks. We had enough that, once, we invited neighbors over for a mini-feast. We roasted a couple of the birds we lost on Black Sunday and served them with hot Irish soda bread. The neighbors brought some home-made beer and greens. We took respite from the storms and hunger, forgot about what hurt us for the span of a meal and a conversation. We had all lost someone or parts of ourselves to the Depression, but I could see then the possibility of something else. Something later. I looked at Janus and saw him smiling and laughing. I felt light enough to float away. I imagined what I'd see if I were above us, looking down on a bunch of tired farmers and their families celebrating something as simple as a meal.

Later that night, after the guests went home and we cleaned up, I tried to tell Janus what I experienced. "It sounds like hope," he said.

My lips trembled at that thought. "Do you still feel guilty?"

"We tried to help her."

"We tried to help Daddy, too, though we couldn't have known then. But do you feel guilty?"

"What do you want me to say?"

"I have more, too. I mean your leg."

"We can still have hope. It's okay to have hope."

I brought the idea of hope to bed with me. I closed my eyes and I saw Margit from behind, her freckled neck and her blond hair pulled up in a fraying bun. In my imagi-nation, Margit turned to me and smiled. A good memory untainted with loss. Happiness. I opened my eyes and opened the window. For a flicker of a moment, I thought of a possible dust storm, unannounced and unwelcome, and what an open window meant in a potentially debil-itating storm. But it was just for a moment; I opened the window wider.

ACKNOWLEDGMENTS

First, thank you to my grandmother Helen Lampkins and my sister Natasha. Wish you were here to see this! My continued thanks to my family: my parents Maxine and Laurence Bellinger, and my sisters Rachelle, and Prudence, all of whom have always instilled in me the desire to follow my goals.

The idea for *New to Liberty* grew under the tutelage of Judy Slater, my friend and professor and the first chapters were written in Timothy Schaffert's novel workshop. Timothy, you have done so much for me! Megan Gannon thought the short story I wrote should be longer, and emily danforth's fire under my ass got the first complete draft done. Thank you! Maud Casey responded to the first draft in her novel writing workshop, and Joy Castro, Jonis Agee, Gerald Shapiro, and Patrick Jones were all important early readers. My awesome office mates Julie Iromuanya, Wendy Oleson, and Arra Ross, were instrumental in discussing writing. I am forever grateful to you all!

Thanks to the University of Nebraska-Lincoln's English graduate program for giving me the time and space to write. Jay Parini, with workshop fellow Melinda Moustakis, read a sizeable early chapter at Bread Loaf Writers' Conference. Thank you to Jay, to Melinda, and to Bread Loaf!

Thanks to Steve Edwards and Rebecca Bednarz for your friendship and support. I'm so fortunate to know you!

Thank you to Olivia Smith at Unnamed Press for your magic. And finally, thank you Alice Tasman for your frankness and constant faith.